I0764421

WAYFARING

Also by John Fraser
and published by AESOP Modern:

Animal Tales

Black Masks

Blue Light / Starting Over

The Case

Down from the Stars

Enterprising Women

Hard Places

An Illusion of Sun

The Magnificent Wurlitzer

Medusa

Military Roads

The Observatory

The Other Shore

The Red Tank

Soft Landing

The Storm

Three Beauties

Wayfaring

WAYFARING

JOHN FRASER

AESOP Modern Fiction
Oxford

AESOP Modern Fiction
An imprint of AESOP Publications
Martin Noble Editorial / AESOP
28 Abberbury Road, Oxford OX4 4ES, UK
www.aesopbooks.com

First edition published by AESOP Publications

A catalogue record of this book is available from the British Library.

First edition 2012, revised 2014

ISBN: 978-0-9572061-1-3

Printed and bound in Great Britain by
Lightning Source UK Ltd,
Chapter House, Pitfield, Kiln Farm,
Milton Keynes MK11 3LW

CONTENTS

Coming in to Land on Saturn

BOY, are we moving fast! Advantage of being trained so taut. And when we hit, cosmic yammo, all perched on spinning balls, comet-dodging, looking for peace – in Lowestoft? Or King City. Well, I mean, what's wrong with that? Came downstairs and dwelt among us; looking for jelly sandwiches in the ice-box. Just ripping off mythologies – only 45, dead on the kitchen floor, seared all over like a waffle. And jeeze boy – was he still travelling when he hit!

Guffaw full of respect. Spies' hangout. Many wife- and ghost-slayers, inner-city spooks, skilled at vaporising in carburettors. Gotta slooow down fore I hit that firewall. One million miles of winds lapping, scent of hydrogen core. Grinding up the beach with surfboard dwindling, scuttering up styrofoam ridges like hares on snowfields. Brother planet arched like an eyebrow, or elephant-moth-caterpillar, defended with these goddam waves, going so fast against me sounding like sound or squeaky treacle. Experience pure: no connection with people living or dead: clean end like clouds belching. All is revealed just too quick and over before the sensor burning out can register.

Might have been a moonflower, cuticle of silverfish. Mooning on, about this really weird job, and boss, the hide and hunt game – something off there, a bit off course ...

*

The boss looked too clumsy, too human. It was a mixed meeting. He chewed on a seegar. 'Men: And other things. And, er, peripherals.'

We operatives took it all in. The human ones unblinking. Other things absorbed with flickers of their liquid crystal eyes. And others, able to digest and crunch more information than there'd ever be in that room, took it all in with a frustrated clatter.

Key words: task, up front, on top. Wallflowers, foxgloves, redhot pokers, Canterbury belles – the chief had been obsessed with English gardens. Our spying roles fitted nicely with homelier flowers. Except, that we were spying on ourselves. Condemned by force majeure to a monastic mumble of key- and last-words, and to celibacy in all things, from head to heels.

'We are,' said the boss, 'temporally between moments; you might say "temporarily".' He stumbled it. 'Spatially, we are behind one thing, and before another. Just past, you could say, but not yet arrived. Not quite here, and not quite there. Not now, but not then, no, definitely not *then*: more waiting, but not exactly *for* anything. We can't assume that when we have waited there will be anything – er – more; other; of the same; different, but similar in essentials. Meanwhile, however, we must all join in thanking you others – and peripherals – for helping in our search and struggles. All join, that is, who aren't mechanicals.'

These stood their ground well. No threatening word had been uttered. In essence, in this odd dimension where the 'extra-dimensional' – as we called them – roamed about, we were lucky to have mechanicals to help. The 'extras' appeared at times in marvellously tiny resolution or in immense, featureless enlargement. As the 'extras' moved towards, away from, and painlessly through us, like so many great, but dead, men, the machines could give us readings. Immense of the tiny ones, minute of the elephantine, so we thought we knew what 'they' were – if rightly one could use the plural. So, the endless furrows of what seemed a huge ice-plain might turn out to be the vast exaggeration of a speck of mica, and what seemed a common beetle to be really an army of millions upon millions of marching things as tall as cedars, bearing flags of nickel and orange. And theirs, I suppose, was help.

*

One of the advantages of being a spy, especially in a precarious place, for one like me *believing* I am dead, is that there is no problem of atonement. Believing, that is, like in fairies, or that 'yes, that *is* my stetson with the bunch of grapes in it.' Truth, the truth of mysteries, like the fading of teddy-bears in colour, then from shelf to cupboard, bonfire (even), to dustbin or to garbage chute – down into janitor Dan's furnace and round the radiators one more time – that's the truth, yes. Drastically recycled.

Report to our controls. Taking a fine, fair robot with me, well-hung with peripherals.

*

Before I killed my wife, I felt remorse. After, only the desire to escape what might be called 'punishment', or equally, rehabilitation She had often tried to kill me, but perhaps in her case the balance between remorse and flight was different.

I did the decent thing: commit suicide immediately after. I threw myself from the window of our apartment. It was on the ground floor, but I could have hurt myself on a stake used to prop up chrysanthemums. When we spelled that word at school, it seemed to combine a sacred beginning and a profane end.

I was surprised the police did not worry too much about my wife's death. Possibly they were fatalists – 'they'll all have to pop off one day' – more likely, because I was a spy. I was a spy for my country. I don't believe in any country but my own, which has a scanty population – one. But it lends itself to the profession of spying. I have always spied – on my parents, on the au pair girls opposite where we lived.

I was taken to the three colonels. They took it in turn to brief me. The briefings were very brief. They have pips on their shoulders, like bison grazing under mulberry trees. I used to think this and then remember colonels don't have pips. They were not very bright, but they were brighter than me. They pressed me to insult them. I succeeded, and lost my first professional spying job. More interesting was the journey into my brain. It was the first time for me but the brain itself was no new invention. My black colonels had already explored it, perhaps even discovered it. I was taken into it with the aid, indeed the company, of an unknown relative, supposedly Irish, but equally possibly Brazilian or Welsh, one Jesus Malarkey.

It was a most complex visit, no match or comparison with Disneyland or other funfairs. What a lot of slutter, of blur and blot, of forgotten Latin and

German, declensions, of nipple-tickling, trains from Victoria.

I asked J. 'Is this really a brain that we're washing?'

'Well, rather walking through.'

'Then, basically, I'm dead; if I'd any children to know of, this is what I'd have left them. It's like when the light goes off. Seeing nothing is boring. The dark makes you fall about and forget where the door is.'

Washing brains can only be a prelude to eating them. I, carrying my country on my back, was – as it were – taken by a gymnastic through the oft short circuits of my brain by – had he understood the term – my amanuensis. Perhaps they paid an archivist to yoke together Jesus and Malarkey. 'None of that Malarkey, bejasus.' Names unearthed, which never would be earthed, ready on tiptoes to call each other out. An archivist, I fancied, with an old Plymouth, finely tuned, perhaps a girlfriend called Fay.

My brain was no hell: no heaven either. Hell of a fine brain you've got there. The two of us, what we found twiddling and fiddling with the springs and levers and the alphabets lying around was what would help me with my spying. *A mystery.* That thing the barber sees when he looks past the customer's head at the next customer, the long-haired future ready – for a smallish sum – to be reduced to the past. A few snips.

Did I kill my wife?

I had always wanted to marry a dead person. All books on art, religion, literature say that the dead enhance the sense of life for the living. When Lord Nelson, patron signifier of so many pubs, gave up his ghost – surely, sent it out and about – Hardy, called upon to kiss those wooden false teeth, must have preferred to gum. Or perhaps, playing safe and forgetting Kismet, hard to do at such a time, realised Nelson had left his fangs safe in the cabin.

Life is indeed a matter of honour. And honour, as we are leading you into the wood, chosen by the family council to acquire a piece of lead within a spot between your dandruff and where the barber stopped – last Saturday – his snipping for a moment, you can hardly refuse. That's life, take another look soon, if you can.

No I didn't kill my wife, she was dead when I married her.

But yes, I was a spy, and I discovered the MYSTERY. It had nothing to do with why there is no sequel to the Bible, why is it a good book and sells so many copies – whereas I, filling pages of couplings, even those of good citizens of Varna, Ontario, though containing love, hate, etc. – would have meagre sales.

When they take you to the woods, think of the money rich people spend on shrinks to know they married mummies: museum talk. Think of not pissing your pants, or worse. Think of Jiminy Cricket, the seven dwarfs, of grass as high as a rhinoceros's eye, and hope they get the deflection, the angle of dangle, right. Irremediably trivial, no sentiment, no humanist stuff for them to get their gums round.

SPYING

I WAS a great spy. Never caught, never killed, prompt with my payments. I met one of my colonels in an African state. We and two floozies were drinking highballs. Later, he said, 'Clang shut the door, corporal.'

I much dislike physical pain, even in scientific measures on my own body. I'm not paranoid, despite being universally persecuted. I have no political convictions as the computer, swiftly riffled through, will show. My spying, though, did involve quite important matters. For self and others. My journey through my brain – or should I say 'through Brain' – with J.M. revealed little. Not without physical reactions, having forgotten to remove my testicles and other sad, unmentionable equipment. Spies are not really serious people. They like a laugh like anyone else. They have to play blow football with Latvian sailors, if required. Elsewhere the sport is moribund. Or do their duty with five-sex majors, graduated from a small college in Wichita, knowing, however, 'what it's all about'. Or as they say in other countries, that something is moving but we don't know what it is. Spies are unserious, and they are idle.

It is the modern way of gossip. Alas, *my* country is no better off for their existence.

Musing thus, I inclined my mind to my colonel. He had changed colour slightly. His knees were bleached – albinism, I think, not camouflage. Not to be accused of prejudice towards the sod, I should say that he was more sodded against than sodden. Lying in bed during the standard childhood, when the milkperson arrived and with a sharp bottle started. I regret that ...

At this point, the *mystery* started to develop. For me. I was hurting. But others knew, or thought they did, that one existed, and that my murder (also of others) was a useful handle for – as it were – nudge and wink, three oranges in line. A bushel basket of nickels somehow to take home when the bar closed.

I had, as a result of the journey through my brain, which also took me outside the pull of gravity (apples, indeed), and time, glimpsed through closed doors this *mystery*. 'I have never seen China, but I can imagine it.' 'Jesus, Hasbrouck, am I drunk or dead …' (a relation of Malarkey, possibly). In a way, that the mystery lay within, even within this process of torture (Colonel freshly graduated from Groton), disappointed me. I enjoy listening to telephone calls, counting bodies, compiling lists of suspects. In fact, I'm only a nice person when I confess and repent. This makes fame and fortune for many, however. Above all, not to blame the century, poor passive thing.

As we swished down the snow, we discussed whether we were driving snows or sleds. I could not get rid of a simple little tune from Maiaskowski and the notion that I had to buy a new (or fresh) pair of trousers. I thought it was unfair to say that peasants don't appreciate nature: perhaps they appreciate their own too much when it comes to putting a rabbit in the pot before its time. When it would say 'stay'. Kept in small cages, like dogs or tiny tigers, they lose that sense of the broader life – peasants, rabbits – that sends us running off foolishly into someone else's yard, instead of quietly creeping into the pan.

Considering rabbit legs in white sauce, I started thinking of the creaminess of old friends forever young, women now, all of them ... Not to give offence: 'I only ever did it twice, with the priest,' one of my little friends once said. How could one respond?

Keeping me hanging there, where the asphalt ends, by the thumbs. Like someone else but she was dead. Who could pity oneself, not pitying others – and so many many of them.

Cities we live in like a double helix. A double zigzagurat, full of pizzerias, jewellers' shops, leather, bakers'. And coming back, alligator handbags, bread shops, jewellery. 'These 'People are mad, star crazy, star craving.' 'Yes, this is the centre of the mad part of the province.' Glad to have only my country on my back.

A chat with my colonel, and my wife.

And after that, there's still the *mystery.*

We went to this country of mauve and silver; often the cities were so small, tourists would buy two or three and leave them in their hotel rooms. They were quite heavy.

'Which side are you on?' asked one of my colonels.

'My country's,' I replied, quick as lumps of lead through the ceiling. All meaningless, hopeless, junked-up twaddle, moralism.

'Aha,' he responded, and rummaged in the lower floors of his head. Oh had he but a guide as fine, as quick with the bottle from the rocket and the cork from the socket, as Jesus Mularkey. Pain repeats itself, and pain repeated is not good for one. From Groton he came, breasting through O-levels, bemedalled already: life gets tired too – 'begat – begat, begat'. Certain situations, involving much digging of holes, confusion, use of pull-throughs and boiling water, fanciful literature, use of sporting facilities for non-sporting ones. Read it in the papers, damned if we do, as they say. Hold a lot of people, stadiums. Nothing against armies myself. Nothing at all.

My colonel wore a cross, and I wondered if he weren't the chaplain, even the Charlie type. Kiss you as you walk off the plane, on the hand, so you don't remember you've no parachute. Too many details obscure the big details. Sharks don't bite if you're bleeding, and if you're dead they don't care, or so they say.

My colonel was pleased with my talk of country and my loyal support. Offered me a code based on Brer Rabbit or Stalky and Co., the only books they had. I chose Brer r., a character not well characterised, though nor was Black Beauty, Tarka the totter, or Wild Fang, if I remember right.

Before dealing with what they really wished to know about, the *mystery*, I shall digress again about the mauve and silver city, quarter as old as time, and the beautiful person, old turkey or gorgeous chick, fine roosting mate, especially after my experience with the enhancing dead.

There was a princess bold enough to kiss the toad on the nose, and which thanking her grew to an enormous toad, twice human size, big as the big voodoo doll, for general use. Kept in the back parlour of the Electric Hoopoe. Hard mouthful for King Stork. My collected buddies were convinced I'd solved the angels on the pin question: 53 large, 79 small – prime numbers indeed – when the question came again (ah sweet mystery).

What is heaven?
When they open the gates to the dead.
What is hell?
When they open the gates to the living.
Who is God?
He who commands.
What does he command?
Faith in he who commands.
What is the simplest operation?
Opening a bean pod.
What is the hardest operation?
Killing a pig.
Who is your neighbour?
He who lives next door.
Who is your enemy?
He who lives next door.
What do you eat?
Pigs and cows.
What will eat you?
Pigs and cows.

We continued in this vein.

In this silver and mauve city, when the sunset comes, it brings with it a touch of gold and of birch brooms. Butterflies, blurry-eyed about the wings, give way to moths, stitched and rolled together from old folios. I took the elevator (we called it the excavator) down to the 30th underground floor. 'Hi, Anna Mae,' I said as though fresh from the manuals of people management. There was no one there. On the screen, the thousand towers appeared, the domes went round, the canapes of purple food went down, the briefcases for home delivery were stacked, ready for ray checking. Hallucinating nicely, Ray.

Mail: the Scottish reeling season is back; swimming is permitted; colonel two needs to speak to you; no foreign objects or personnel down the elevator shaft. The shredders started working. It snowed at finger-warmth. It's always all gone in the morning. Who knows what throws it down? Could be Wall Street. In the morning – nothing. Only the heating. turned up a bit so's we know it's winter. Then – an agent zapped; in one country, a rabbit plague we started. In another a rabbit plague we didn't. This way we shall never find our personalities. Export poverty and riches, and at home the highball, ball-game: jog and sleep.

The real mystery we didn't find through spying, driving in twilight, morning and night. The winking cross over the city – **REMEMBER THE BETRAYED/BETRAYERS** – grand crucifixion of bulbs.

Revolving gardens full of plastic. The twilit shops. My colonel, instead, under mountains of rabbits. 'Why the hell do anything so silly?' Just an idea that worked.

Anna Mae? Where can she be? Personnel don't keep addresses. Invades our privacy and spreads gossip. So no one knows. We can't ask the police – we are the Police, the super-cops. A small seminar with unknown persons: subject of rabbits, plague, surplus, or plaything. Usual remarks. Plaything not very much remarked on. Plague seen as a better bet then food. No Anna Mae. Lunch, a bitter salad with potato skins, some dry rice which broke my crown – dentist all the afternoon, reading the chinchilla ads in the antechamber.

Mysteries: don't believe in them myself – but where is Anne Mae? Why do they talk here of the dragons coming out of the lake (hairy, forked tail, black as night and so on)? What are they after? Why is it always twilight here, a twilight all the more pressing as we must dim our lights to save – energy. Why is the other city – the green and gold one – which spirals up our own, never touching, never illuminating, ever more obscure, distant, and yet so much brighter than our own?

In our training as spies we did everything. Took all drugs, submitted to all intimidations, tortures – as you know – read all ideologies. And in the end, we had to commit all crimes. At least since my wife was dead I could get off with an easy murder, but other things we had to do were nasty. The sexual ones did not too much concern me, but the burning and kidnapping, cheating at cards, signing in at hotels with stupid names (three D. Ducks at one time in the bridal suites of the same motel) – made me sad and uncomfortable. Report read '... indelible belief in own badness which in reality is just naughtiness and sentimentality pared to the bone'. In the service we recognised the logic and swapped our loves like poker or potato chips. Everything has its logic. But why that, not this? Why this person, idea, city, not that?

We had to keep indoors and go out only when it was really twilight by our watches. In summer we were cool and dim, in winter dim and warmer. In the evening when we worked indoors, it was bright, and warm and cool according to the season. Spying is not so dangerous – worse is being spied on. My colonel and I were linked together like two schoolboys joined by plastic earphones and a length of twine. Few important words, and many lost. Spying, they said, is not by and on anyone, but a profession and a skill, conducted at minimum cost to oneself and maximum to one's employers. That city was squalid: limbo, farm girls, cruising, ripe, easy picking.

The dragons from the lake are classical. Long nose like a wolf's, forked tail, hair all over, smelling of sulphur, worship of Manitou. Why come out of the lake? The drug course was hard, but I passed it. Guerillas were easy.

Where is Anna Mae?

'Got the 'flu,' said someone. One mystery less.

The great mystery, of life, and spying to keep our little bit going, doesn't interest me. Rather, the city interests me. Elevators which do as they want, go up and down. Lights all day; the processors, human and mechanical, who work all day: the human ones go out to buy checked pants, the plastic ones await their new program. Who grumbles the most? I can't take off my pants, but the twirling beasts in the corridor shamelessly spit out their tapes.

We had problems with the geese. The lights attracted them, and the twilight kept them. Then, as the reader knows, we had trouble with the robots. Victorious over the human species, they said. All shapes and sizes. Only thing they couldn't do was dance and eat a horsemeat steak in Brussels Midi. I was just a leaden soldier, ready for the button-mould. Robots couldn't find Anne Mae – indifferent too to free tickets for the opera. In the late and early light you couldn't find people. Mind silting up. The robots refused their food. At times, the lights went off.

Collecting things was one answer – teddy-bears, miniatures or Anna Maes or chocolate boxes.

I collected something, too. I had lumps all over, and insomnia. Company doctor looked at my leg, and said, 'That'll have to come off,' 'The leg?' 'The lump,' he said, the leg will follow. Waved aloft, I thought. All red and blotchy.

'Is your job stressful?'

'Intelligence. That's why I'm here.'

'Do you smoke?' asked he. No.

'You're lucky, I've only got one left.' My cure, then.

'Only with a prescription. From security. They don't give them any more.' Give me a prescription, then.

'Shakespeare said we'd end up with three legs, so losing one would be rejuvenating.'

I said: 'Can I have a second opinion?'

'Yes. You don't need your leg chopped off. And here's a third – half chopped. Ever had it off when you were half cut?' We smirked at his sally. He had a good deskside manner,

I went to see my colonel. He wanted me with lumps all over. Three things were lacking, all my fault: dates for all hips and whores of the city. Big crates of parts for killer-craft not yet delivered. War-news breaking down into cheap repartee.

'If you're intelligence,' he said, 'you should know there's a mystery brewing. I can get you a new recruit. But she'll have to go through security.'

'Called Anna Mae?'

'Yes, but now you've blown your new recruit. If you knew who she was, she's no security.'

'She never had much here.'

'Do you smoke?' Yes, I said.

'Pity, it's the last one,' he laughed and lit it.

We communicated well. I could never do what he wanted.

They had turned the lights down further. It was happy hour, and I fumbled my way to the company bar. With the current so low, the elevator takes an hour to go down thirty floors. No one comes up. We're not supposed to know names, and letters and numbers are off-putting at drink time. We make up our own – Kapuskasing, Dognose, Gavi. Sometimes they called me M'larkey, sometimes kedgeree – a dish I'm fond of, but have never tasted.

Sweet misery of life. We called the colonels waistcoat, digger and wassail. The first put his chums in cement waistcoats, the second in his flowerbeds. The third because we once offered him a beer: he asked 'Wassail?! They were not the key.

If I lose my legs, how can I hunt – conventionally – the mystery? Should we first ask, perhaps, where are we? Our city now seems invisible. If you can so easily helix one inside another, zigzag one mystery about another, who knows how many continents you can pack into Australia, how many bits of persons and whole persons, transit cars, rails, trucks, wagons, ox-carts they have slipped into each one? So much memento mori of trucked freight.

We are not bright. Without the Building, we would accomplish little. Everyone who enters the Building is enslaved by it. The rain came in, and there was a to and fro of shredders, processors, archivists. I ramble on. We are not bright, and it is better so. We do not serve power, we are not power, we do not trouble ourselves with what 'it' is. We make lists, we inform to inform to inform.

But I know there is a mystery. I have read widely in the history of the Bourbons, and of codes of honour in the larger islands – Ireland, Sardinia, Sicily, Corsica, Crete, Malta, Rhodes. Honour among thieves is a phrase which much attracts me. But robbery? Hurting? Not much. I have seen fear in a fly's eyes: 120 of them. If you catch two at it – 240: eyes down: the eyes have it. We had no flies with us: not even on the standard issue pants we got from the company. There was some kind of sticky plasticated zip, on the lines, I suppose, of not being caught with one's pants down, though what good this did I do not know. Most people who spy are quite incurious. They don't even want to know secrets. I do. I'm different from the others. And we're all different from the poor prisoners and hostages who get caught. We're free.

THE MYSTERY

BECAUSE I like a mystery, they asked me to go and find out what it was. There are three levels – I'll explain. First, details. To have the warrant for the other city, where there is other light, the green and the gold duly mowed and polished every morning. They have a special kind of cat, grey-blue, fur an inch long. They sit in the gardens, and are unhindered. They watch the transit system which I shall use, with my pre-prepared travel warrant, but without the pre-packed poisonless spies' lunch, which I felt it infra-dig to eat in public. Especially as my mission (I call it the mystery tour, or the treasure hunt), whilst of basic importance, is of no special importance to anyone special. Besides, those little packets of plum cake, dates, pemican, sultanas, cauliflower rendered to dust, leave oneself so healthily full of vitamins and survival that one loses the sense of death. For that, as I sped past the cats and the gardens full of arum lilies and canterbury bells, is a sense we have in our city, now hidden by the helix of this new one.

The other levels were 'find' and 'fetch'. Now I was at level one: 'run'. First, then, to call my colonel and tell him I was on mission, dropping in on anyone my mandate allowed. Swift city transit systems go fast, and I could tell him I was already in Central Africa before my ticket had run out. I could say there were giraffes, long trunks, big snouts in and under water. Not true. Gas stations, abattoirs for horses, old Plymouths – usual 1/2/3 world stuff. Wish I'd taken my poisonless lunch. Or looked up an old friend who once shot a bear on his fridge.

'She has arms which don't reach her elbows,' someone said to me in Italy. If you really want to reach the mystery, you have to discover the mystery, bend your elbows, hands in pockets, let your arms reach your knees, if needs be. Chopped-up street corner thoughts.

I know where the mystery lies, and I'm sorry they did not pick me till after so many years with Anna Mae, my dead wife, and all the sweet old bureaucrats. It lies in the three levels – our city, what we do, and what it's all about. Problem to connect them.

In the meantime, I got five bulls and a teddy by trying the gun with the misaligned sights. It's my trade, and the sighting shot tells you all, especially if the manager isn't looking. Otherwise you pay twice. Practise three times a day on the range. Small arms expertise I have. Hate to see animals and people suffer. Horrible, Pointless. Lots of sounds that sound alike, making little holes in cards or people. No point. They say when the next bout of rain arrives, in America they've lots of arks, underground, animalless, packed with experts.

The train beckons, so does my colonel. Think of cat with dusty paw, fishing in a glass of Pinch, for non-fish.

*

The transit system went to its end, and when we stopped we were in another country. Bustling out, greasy sandwiches in Christmas-presented briefcases.

It was also a port. I went to a bar. They were plying faro. At the table was a witch. I like witches (if they like me), and she could play faro well, and was passably beautiful. I don't have the head for cards, but she was a witch, and I have the eye for them; they know, and appreciate it.

'I'll call you Streh, if you don't object; I don't have a name as I'm on mission, as you knew. I don't think you want to call me Jesus, but M'Larkey sounds a bit coarse. Call me Fra', because I'm between one place and another. But what country is this?'

'The end of the transit system,' she said without enthusiasm. She won a hand. 'How did you know I was a witch?'

'How did you know I was a spy?'

'Are you a white one or a black one?'

'My boss is black.'

'So?'

Someone came in, one of the busy messengers who make everyone uneasy. Done it, he mouthed; cost me a leg but they'll come. Later, when I was in bed with Streh – too bad by the hour a change of sheets is not included, and we agreed that mutual masturbation was healthier for our tastes than closer contacts – she said two interesting things. First, that in this country there was a trade in mysteries, like cargo cult, but without the waiting. Secondly, that the people really were arriving. I had a nasty feeling that Dognose might be one of them, which would mean I was being followed, or was following him.

'Well, Fra', you've finished. Time to pay.'

'Just one thing – first, are these secrets or mysteries? Secondly, in what do they consist?'

The people had arrived. With Streh's help I became very lean and flat, and slid under the door. Rolled into a cylinder, I easily fitted the keyhole of the next room – thus avoiding cleverly both paying the bill and using my noisy spy tools to force the lock. We spies have a myriad of such tricks. Being lifelong sleepers, being in two places, being in no places, taking photographs of Swiss destroyers in the Caspian. I won't explain how we do it, but we have a thorough and perhaps unique training. They teach us to make up stories, to while away a year or so when we have destructured.

Harriet and her horse:

Harriet was a lissom young girl. Her father was a rich stockbroker with offices in Denver and the Cotswolds, but he was so rich he sat all day in front of his terminal and watched the cash flow in, or not. One day, Harriet said 'Doodlepops, Doodlepoops, can I please have a horse?'

And her father said: 'Don't call me Doodlepoops, yes and leave me in peace.'

So she got her horse. She neglected it a bit, but the man with the field looked after it till it died.

Alternative ending:

'Daddy, can I have a horse?'

'No. Don't call me Daddy. You must earn the money. When I was your age I'd already inherited my first million.'

So Harriet went into the bathroom, and tried on her first lipsticks, settling for a nice purple colour, with a light black line around its glossy surface. Then she stood on a corner of Frith Street, and was soon very successful. Lots of men offered her chocolate and things generally bad for the liver, but she was quite a businesswoman and wouldn't even accept credit cards. Sometimes she worked the little cinemas, and sometimes she went into clubs – she always got in free because she said she was looking for her daddy. She always came out with one. Soon, she had enough for her horse; in the course of business she had met a super trainer, who never took off his little trilby. He thought it would go well over jumps, but they found a super little jockey, who told them they knew nothing. So they raced it at an evening meeting at Windsor. It went like a cracker, but owner's orders were to let Harriet pick up something on another nag, so it slowed down, much to its annoyance when the driver seemed to lose interest. It won a plate or something somewhere in the North, and then lost badly over a mile. It came in third to nothing at the second Goodwood meeting. 'That's about it.'

But by now Harriet had a keen eye for all kinds of flesh. So they put it in for a big race at its distance, going, jockey told to pay attention, everything. It went like a cracker. The favourite was still standing when it swooped round the bend. But then it rather blew up, and finished last. So Harriet sold it, and it looks very nice hacking round Hyde Park.

*

Gone the hope of using one of the tricks – the flying to the highest tree, the hiding in the cracked tile, the night presence by the emperor's bed. I could not move from mine. Next door, they were mumbling in an organised way. They had heavy footfalls. Who were they? Christian souls? Impossible question. At times they broke off, perhaps to ask themselves just that. Then they went on, a flock with rustling fleeces, backsides facing into the same wind.

A man comes in. He is fumbling with his clothes, as though not used to wearing them, or others. He looks martial. I picture him in a wreath, tending to shrubs outside the temple of war and peace. He kicks me just below the bony part of my chest. I picture him in a cuirass, with metal muscles. He kicks me just below the sternum, but not as though he wants to find out anything. I was not hurt, just anxious. In my job, one spends a lot of time being dead. Being kicked makes me wonder if he knows his job. Let's hope he's not a sadistic nurse, or a doctor.

'Is this a hospital?'

No answer. A bronzish face, rough like the inside of a bell, an Indian who spends too long indoors, or an Englishman too long out. He asks,

'Do you want mysteries? Things I know and you don't, or what neither knows?'

He just wants something big. 'The most mysterious thing is the human body,' I venture.

'Not much of yours left.' An idiot. With a key. But I don't want to escape. I don't know where I am. My witch helped me hide among paper clips, clusters of bats, familiar things sized differently. But the unfamiliarity of a real dumkopf ... If I roll over, he can't kick me in the chest. But there's the liver, black ash though it is. And over again – up come the kidneys, though.

They had me down: my private pre-war over. Body not answering questions. Mystery down to name and number, beat and drip. Not much of me left. Retorts inside an amphora, some running hot, others fizzing slowly, ooze of ochre, brown and red, streaks here and there of green – turquois or shagreen, green-veined with green so dark it could be dry. Need lots of amphoras to stand each other up – now, I'm on a bed. No brain, just a stopper, leaded down. No, can't be lead – to breathe need cracks, nose not full of odour, mouth like a rose, whiskers – exec. issue, tobacco and lobster trickling sweetly down to the ear. Swirling there like summer dresses, store-dressed for dirty little girls, pat the cow but mind, the cow pats – bits of eggshell ... But no! not eggshell, teeth, mine, only ones allowed in here, mouth that seems too small for all the things I had to pack. Packed in a hurry, tongue and things thrown in, strapped down but lolling out.

I'm not too well. Fall? Wrong diagnosis? Light fires beneath the kidneys – devil them, the brave last words. Words can be brave, but suppose, instead of boat and boatman, there's a toll-bridge? With a plastic card I didn't bring, to let one in: should have got one from supplies. Though I must say, the place is probably all swamp, ripe and overripe mangoes, out of reach. And all those books – 'You'll never tire ...' For all ages, 'You'll never tire of bridge .. or barbie dolls ... or opera highlights ... or pecan Pete's melon pies...' 'Heaven is when they open to the dead, hell, to the living.' Under the mangroves, see the little groups just ... never tiring. Isn't that The Pearl Fishers? Isn't that an ankle strap? Isn't that a pumkin pie and 10¢ gas? Isn't that four no? It all depends on the four of hearts. The cards never tire, either.

The soldier nurse reads my mind; its loops and bumps came out on long rolls of paper, inked in by longlife fountain pens.

'You have very simplistic ideas of what is mysterious,' he said.

Where he kicked me is coming up in ugly lumps, like mulberry fruit, purple, trodden on.

'Forget about those,' he says. 'There's a duel tomorrow. You're the star. I'll get you nice new clothes. The tailor'll size you through the spy.'

Textiles have always lent themselves to sweating, and I sweated. Empty of remorse, but not alas remorseless, and utterly unlikable but not unlike: standard size, in fact. Clothes for my little body. Remember the undertaker, when we had to file the chief: 'Sir, we do not line our boxes, we stuff them.' Funny job, stuffing caskets for the chief, ring with black stone, wouldn't come off the finger, – which, instead, would. They wanted 'hail to the chief' for him, but the guys he drank with said it would be vulgar. His favourite was 'everything's coming up roses and daffodils' – at least, he hummed or mantraed that while opening mail, but again – veto. Not apt. So we trundled him along to bits of Wagner the organist had; Siegfried Idyll, while we were waiting for him, Rhine journey up the aisle, and then on tape a piece of the Dutchman while they cooked him. Never much thought of death, as institutions go. Too much hit and miss, and no time to get into the right mood. A duel, now, that was something else; or rather, it was the same thing, but an operative could have some honour and respect in it.

No one was in the garden. I was wearing a greyish shroud. I felt like the voice of the Lord God, before being made flesh. Dwelling among no one. No banana leaves for A, no socks and shoes for the snake, no his and her leaves for E. I wonder if they were all *fat*, obese. Nothing to do, and the Lord God seems to have had a sweet tooth – milk, honey, manna, bees' nests. Two plumpish prudes with nothing to do, and a lone python with no one to do anything with.

The garden was free of weapons. Except perhaps there had been a scythe, to cut off the lid of the stalk-mouse's nest – full of pink wrigglies, exposed. North wind came up – from where, the sea? – through clay vents in the walls, too high for captive breezes. Yes, it must be the sea, buckling and folding down there and sending up a little mooing clifftop air. Garden is like they used to be, Italian, a bit worn-through: gourds among nastertiums, foxgloves fencing back the lilies, all kinds of bells and lanterns, the early-morning, scenteds, fine weeds like oats, once-flowering roses cut down to poppy-size, all kinds of poppy – pink, silk-red, white and purple. Butterfly yellow, purple, white; a green and silver snail; lizard with discrete studs all over. All birds down; or moving forward like a stalking game when no one is quite looking – at cones, a burr, dry cow-parsley heads, fallen red apples. Birds coloured under, turning back to brown and silver-grey, under all fire or blues of arcs or waterfalls. All bricks hot with lead and sulphur, hollyhocks, all cushion-cover, temperament coming out, not nodding, lower flesh dark, mushy, nearly black. Expect to find some wooden chairs, mock-Chinese china gravy boats, for superstition among the granite chips, colours of meat – beads of a necklace, green bottle-glass; wild oats, and purple heads of maize, iris – lines, drawn with unshaking hand.

Mulberry-tree: fruit like my wounds, but maggots busy. And what the sound says – whoom, whoom, up through the conduits, notched at the lips as though with shells, clay or dough; says nothing. Is for itself, let go, the fountain dry, no primal cart, the wheelbarrow, sign of techne and love combined, full of freshly-rendered sheep shit. The tender, unwarlike wheelbarrow – never used for trickery, taking a city, hiding a messiah – useful for wheeling leaves, geraniums in triumph. Just yellows grass as it keeps warm all winter, lain on its stomach, then springs up long and green, dodging out in springtime, when it's up and off again.

Here, there's no gate, no compost heap, no rake. It all does for itself. What duel is this? With flowers, air, morning waits? Gardens must wait, there's nothing else to do. If it's a duel, I must have lost. There's no one here; no door, and so I could not have got in. Not a mystery, just an impossibility. I'm not here, then. Just lie on this plank, wait for the snake of gardener. Smells nice. Too many cells – the bees dance before the hive because they don't want to go back in. Perhaps I'm supposed to dig, or cut a pipe to smoke or play, measure the azimuth, get away. But since I can't be here, there's no away to go to. No E. and so no snake, no leaves to lift, no skulls to crack, no appetite – the apples do look rather sour. No danger. Check my hair – just fine: no fear from eagles bearing tortoises. Too much spying wore me out. If anyone comes, he can't be here either. Simplest answers really *are* the best. Cut through the mystery to the mystery within. First time for ages I've felt really safe, here where I'm not.

*

Back in the cell. There I can be. It has a door. It is a gentle spot, though. Except for the kicking. Though I can't go out, they can come in only three times a day, and then for five minutes only – special locks. Come from Maryland, fine craftsmen, make the same thing for you in wood; a ward, I wonder, in wool or silk, a fine linen prison, like a sail. Finely stitched upon it, all of us – and no one's come but nursie: stitched, I should like to think, by brothers in their cells. Long chains of circumstance from bee to architect, long sentences with finer points delayed, but we all, finely embroidered, bravely bellying out. I like that 'bravely bellying': judging by the food, and even nursie's manner, part screw, part minister, could be monastic something here. But what thing? At least I've modified the door. If Streh comes, there's no door problem. She is in rooms, not in and out of them.

No sooner said than done. You can't go very far in rooms. At least, you soon come up against the space problem. And so I left the room, not through the door, into a corridor. Rightly sounds the premiss to other doors, or still to outdoors, or to coridas – places which only lead to others similar, or spaces between, like air-bricks in walls, which are really walls, not air at all.

*

The run down was not too frightening. Where there are no sides, there can be no bottom. We passed through sandflats, mudflats, seven seasides of sandpipers and oystercatchers, each sea a different smell, armies of birds, all interrupted. At times an echelon would sheer off – mechanical tilt. Nursie – but now I called him officer – had come along. More time-space lounging by. Such a lot of things lost up here – small souls like bytes in the big machine: the kind of thing we thought about in training camp ... They picked the narcissists, and then removed the bits of personality that clung to us. 'Whatever happens, resist any attempt to provide you with a personality. Hang in with yourself. Be curious about everything. But don't get mixed up in things, in people.' That's why Streh was so good for me. She could hide in the lining of a drawer, thin as a cigarette paper, for two centuries, knowing she'd be found. 'Nothing to waste but time – that's what I call real luxury.' It was true. She could have taken the 'stuff' – roadsters and phaetons, toadstones and amethysts: 'trash' she called it. And now here it is, all round us, reconstructed into crystals, battery-plates, hooves, solid tires, lengthened hems, bundles of undelivered letters.

'In hell there is no danger ...'

Officer went on: 'So this is not hell. But as there are many countries, many brothers, may there not also be many hells?

'Only one death, but reached by many roads, singing on some, on others torpid in wheelbarrows.

'Here, however, there is no danger, and if you prefer it, life. Some of the rules don't hold, is all. Your colonel, I see, has given you up. He knows you're only interested in spying, in finding out. Any secret will do, if it has a keyhole. Matching the dance of atoms, censoring letters, writing your own and not posting them, that's secrecy, that's the real banality for you. The drama which is as banal as the banal. The hidey-hole we've all used. You don't want sex, even the mistletoe bough is boring. You find the box you can't get out of: a few kisses and you're stifling. You don't care why it's boring. Because you know it is, you just want to know how. Accepting your own death, that of others is no concern: it's just like your own. Acceptance is existence, and acceptance is the only real knowing between two infinitely long black corridors. What could be more banal than this postcard? Or being flat as a board?'

The card was from my colonel, I felt sure. I tried to see the address, where I was. But of course, it might not have come to me direct. But then – it seemed quite direct. This girl had brought it, lending the personal touch. Kindly touch of chance – like parachutes. Try them out with pigs, one in 500 – instant sausages, but parachutists do much worse.

No news is no news. Have lived through years of terror: kidnappings, bombing strangers in the street, shooting of post-officer clerks. Disillusioned. Didn't bring them new life, nor anyone. Lots of years in jail, repentance, moralism, solipsism. Slow drip of stones on intellect. Still I wanted to find out – and what it was they wanted. Vicarious death, or sport. I am the fly: squash. And then?

What I am interested in – aside from what happens in this city, jail, convent, however it seems – is gadgets, especially bio-gadgets. Aside too from oddities like polishing small things (seeds, avocado pits) to see if something has been written on them. Bio-gadgets as ways of reducing. Society no longer attracts – save as flat leaves one might stick together, possibly to hide under, or as wallpaper. It's hard to see it, yet it sticks out all over. Society needed to be preserved. From what – scuff-marks, pencil slips, blobs of nothing much that might turn out to be Streh, dormant.

Memory all there, written down in language. Self-love, stack of trophies too small to mount – the fly I killed in '59. Perhaps voyaging its journey in the opposite sense – reincarnations as tracts of weeds or algae, very small, travelling through angels' tunics. Defence of freedom, and of me. Could write a book of her, bound in dragon-skin. Into the room where someone else was – a record, some strings. (Not Streh, Streh's a slut, remember.) Shoulders smelling of the sun. Stained glass everywhere. Must be fun to make, but not to be inside, like in a forest; not deceiving peasants, that blue unnatural, out of all nature – sermon taking prussic blue from wrist-bone to the finger's point. Organ unfolds its wings, steering out of its case like clockwork. Cathedral a big time-engine, all seasons in the glass, the wood: dead, stone trees, a calendar with no events, a year without an order, death in the spring. Angels chatter: think deeply of profane things. Bits of bottlebottoms fuse together, glazed bowls all fused. Over all married together. Mountain meadows, before the day is dead, the dew burnt off.

Name without apostrophes, not like that slag – the streg'. Quickly, fit together bits of warm flesh, speed down the rails, two steels oiled, like a sextant's track. Hot afternoons; shoulders casually incised by straps. Mouth roast beef and gravy, powder like pollen, heavy on the back legs. Lovely girl, borrowing your youth. In the travelling cell: just a tube. Must have cost lots.

'We have information that may be useful,' he says. I say,

'Last night I dreamed of grass; too many ants to lie down in it – two chamois running up the edge, scuts like a clump of white poppies.' Make them feel humanity.

'We can help you.'

What a lot they spend to help: or not. Tape recorders, men doing nothing on street corners. Expenses. Male world, women to pick up the pieces: some trained too to shoot someone. Photos of crowds; officer up there, armed. Everyone important, for a buck or two, porters, too.

Memo: requisitions. Accredited agents. Rocks for righteousness, rubber bullets, then melting ones, like suppositories. Pack them with vitamins, for use in poorer districts. Or martinis for the rich. Do you call this friendly persuasion? Think of a very big, or very small, expensive thing. Tap tap. Design for red button 37E. Defend my way of life, I'm paying for it. Blinis;

lamp with apricots; my pewter mug, my old dad and his old dog, pig-swilling here; then the brown-out, rueful, after the life – 'in my new pants.' Up to Stop 33; Brazilian barman, experimenting all the afternoon – purple, green and amber. Joke about flags. Knows I'm with the Service, or a drummer: spirit of '76: fighting for the likes of him. Paper bags on heads of suspects. Remember to get the steaks; biodegradable; let them eat paper bags. Language-disc in place: 'Waddya mixin' there, Xavy? 'nother lizard-killer?'

'No Sirree', (film talk), 'thisun's here's a remedy for sour 'gators.'

Fine use of apostrophes, zero for composition. Small, nicely coloured black. Might do for the collection. Continental blobs on sheets. Too corny: bar operators. **RUN IF FILE THETA**. Must look you up, sometime. Caught between two chips. Archive on gelatine, some millions of ketchup freckles, lethal chambers on the stomach – instant dissolves, on contact with gut juice. 'Gimme a 'gator juice, Xavy.' Keep them all stirred up. Down there in the snowy street, all-weather tinted glass, a kind of gold, makes snow look burnt, the grass looks white – magnificent suns. Sad bums wandering in the snow. Silver dollars sunk in bar top. Try to lift one out, authentic gold reflection. Copies.

Pay us to be beastly to you. Professional pigtail-pullers, users of catapaults and moon bombs, big shiny packets full of things to lick. Ow! Kicked my books right out from under my arm there. Nasty, dirty books. Man with dirty fingernails wrote them; thin hand, poor circulation.

'We're from the FBI.' Looking up, looking me up, and down. 'Oh yeah, boys, waddya sellin' this week.' Think of that little slip of DNA that has to go on, when they've run my tiny plastic chart. Binomial agent, spread out defenceless, the mannikin outside the restroom, always laughing. Must see an awful lot. They've got something on me. Absolute end. Fiddling expenses, leaving street corners, paying agents twice, continuing to requisition for the dead. Not dead, just moving on through. Agent held, not holding, just re-taken on. Worth it, my way of life.

'Gee, this is some classy bar.' Lame experimental tat. Even pay you to take out the garbage. Found goosebreast in my soup. Usually take it out to make the next batch with, or eaten by the night shift. Squabbling to carry a small portion of the chief's casket. Hands clasped over perforated stomach, holding a fine cigar. 'Got a match, you fellers?'

Naughty. Incredibly classy punishments. Rid guilt of one death by saving lots more: humbug. Monastery garden, made for confession, only no one there: it is my way of life too.

Spill of arms and legs down a transit tube. Non-disagreeable feeling of being drawn and quartered under anaesthetic.

*

'Well, chief, I came back. And I got the mystery.'

Mumble of greed and jealousy. Jumble of bites bitten off and bytes tumbling, promotions deferred, sideways shunts, press-release.

'Gee, fantastic.'

Shooting miles of membrane; torture in a monastery garden, souvenirs disappointing from a matchless country. The finest hour, shedding one form for another – feeling the new wings and legs sliding out of the dry pod. And darlings, what wings, what colours, what powder ...!

'What did you get for us?'

'I saw – it's the best thing for friends and foes. I saw it at first hand. It's made a great difference to me. Made all those tubes and isolations worth while, wrong way down the spiral, slipping in and out of printers' pies.'

'OK – spill it then. What did you bring back?'

'The mystery and its resolution. The puzzle and the how-it-is.'

'The works?'

'Right on.'

'And it's ...?'

Smoking a big cigar, big enough for two. Phone that winks how many friends aren't calling you.

'It's death. I saw it. Take it with you.'

A shy laugh, he gives. A slight loss of virginity. Where's it gone?

'That's it?'

'Yes. They've got it. And I've seen mine. It's not that bad, but pretty final, and I don't want it, not just now.'

'That's *all*? You mean, that's it? And all that money ...'

'What more could you have got? The rest we already knew, – it's all in the books.'

What they didn't have and didn't know about, was Streh. As I left the last big castle, I found her in a pile of old leaves, lying like a pencil-mark on a piece of crumpled paper. Not much to be done to her in that state. Perhaps she'll decide to straighten herself out a bit. Fill out. But she doesn't think in those spans.

'But we had that figured out. We could stretch life and still zap them.' Chief again. No longer dead and buried.

'No, making immortal agents isn't the bother. Sure, I can go on for ever, changing shape and form; a hair of the brush, then the painted I of the VII in an old master clock: the 'd' in a dear John letter somewhere in an attic in Wisconsin ... The problem doesn't lie with life – that comes by itself. It's death.'

*

The sun was rising – and setting – as I stepped out into the twilight. They took my badge, and my trick chip. They stripped out the language programs from my tongue (bit of a nip there with the pincers). Brought up to be tortured means sacrificing a bit of oneself, but it also means to be a little important.

They didn't find Streh. They took my form-changer, so I couldn't slip through the person-processor onto the subway as I usually did. I had to buy a ticket. But this is the nicest time; in the double city, when evening and morning are coming. The streets are covered with chrysalises and dead day-moths, cadmium, Krems white, dragon, lilac powders. True, no job – but the mystery, and its secret!

Rome, 1985

Sometimes the Watchman Is Drunk

THE WATCHMAN had a belly problem, and more directly a pistol problem. He was full of beer and piss and puke, and he sat amidst his needs and desires, and looked and felt good. But his .38 dug holes in him when he stuck it in his waistband. He kept sticking it in and taking it out. I hoped he would not put it on the table, in reach of his drunk and depressive friend. He put it on the table.

'My folks came from here,' I said to him in Albanian. There were two dancers, one in green with sequins who looked angry, and one in a swirling red dress which she twirled to show there was a black eagle on her back. It was an Albanian flag she wore. The watchman said 'They are *the best*' – but not to me.

A year later the bar was closed, no songs, no dances: 'gone to the cemetery' said the notice of closure. I asked two very brown men with a dancing bear, 'What happened to the watchman?' and they winked and said, 'No Albanians here.' The bear was small, not much taller than a man.

The whole province was hot, jiggering and smelling of nutmeg, like a hot pepper on a hotplate. I went north to Titograd, hoping I wouldn't find what I was looking for.

'Fuck it,' I thought. 'There's Jack,' in a bar in Titograd, the body unmistakably seallike, but the hand grasping attention, determined to touch his interlocutor. Macho American pose, intent on proving how real guys can touch you and show their body hair without compromising themselves. Pathetic, perhaps. Jack had financed his politics with drugs, his drugs with politics. But he had reformed, it seemed, prefectly assimilating into Montenegrin society, no longer campus radical and hophead, champion of causes, agent undercover for good – and evil. To my regret, I had found him, after so much trouble: 'If on a winter's night a traveller ...' Here he was, the odious bastard, my brother, my friend.

For a long time he denied being Jack. He had not changed over twenty years, so that I doubted that anyone could look so like one's mental image of them. This simulacrum even had the same tattoos inside his wrist – a tiny elephant, like a horse with a broken head-rope dangling like a trunk: a cat, naif like a jaguar, half a mouse. I drank with him all evening, a roomspan away: I felt good. I'd found him. He looked maudlin, and depressed. In the end he denied knowing me, calling more and more people round to vouch for him. 'OK, Jack, you're not Jack,' I said.

And he said, 'Nor am I who I say I am,' and with that I could have led him away, anywhere, with me. But we were full of beer and vinjak. I tried armwrestling him, but we nearly rolled on the floor. As I righted myself, I glimpsed beneath the table a colony of insects – tiny, mixed shaped, like moving candies in miniature, flavours of all jewels, just shining, furtive complexity of shared tasks and intentions. The beauty of it so intense I remembered journeys with the real, the other, Jack. Travels to the centre of the world, its roots, in rain forests, rivers wide as seas, water running like talking ants.

'I have a job for you, whoever you are,' I said.

And 'Fuck it,' said Jack.

*

His voice, his poodle hair, same bracelet, hand clamped on glass as he leaned towards, over you. Are they all here, then, his cronies? None gone to prison, as they would have done in England, all. US class system works like that: all, perhaps not aged, they Montenegrinised, and vice versa here: little house on the prairie translated to TV, signs for SENDVICI, HAMBURGERI, mixed media, and he had a classy woman with him too, seeming thus unlike himself, his Jackness. Smelled of cinnamon, she did. I sniffed at her (and afterwards she laughed at me, with me, for this).

I insisted we head back South. Asking directions in someone's driveway, standing on a dead dog, almost a skeleton, unburied, unremarked. People again the colour of earth, minarets waiting for blast-off, sky pilots, muezzin calling for countdowns hidden by porch lights, sets flashing violet, arsenic green and Martian orange. Remember a girl in Kichevo – experience very intense, but very, very fast: intimacy (if it was intimacy) not recognised next day. Kichevo: almost the margin of the margin. Only the dogs were amused. Houses made of trees and clay. Remember the Red Army man, who giggled as he took the stage, and danced the girl's part, in his poor uniform. Running to the margin – escape from central horror and the seriousness. Is one pushed there, to the margin, or can one invent, inhabit and people it?

Driving South. Always reminds me of America, and my primal scenes. Car nearly hits a tortoise, high-stepping. village devoted to making hanks of string. Old mudhole, old clothes. Jack and his Anna, hanging on. Jack saying 'for Christ's sake', 'why *here*' 'why the hell *me*?'

Dogs barking – a terrible sound, the bark, without a tongue. Cinema Partizan. Closed cinemas: one evening sat and watched, the reels were mixed, and always Jack 'for Christ's sake, I mean'. Remember as a kid, this girl, we walked and walked, till we came to a Micmac's home, with a pickup trucks outside, Jean Tremblay it said on the side. And me saying, 'I didn't know you was an Indian.'

And she, 'What you think I am then?'

And me, 'I kind of liked – I liked your kind of face', and voice, and indignation, and way of speech: did then, and still do.

'We have arrived,' I told them. Ruined Elizabethan cottages, in a long thin line. Snooker rooms; barbers shops, cake shops, hanks-of-string shops. Rural petit-bourgeoisie. Three customised cars with German plates and racing tape, attempt at love lights.

Kerbstones pink marble, little spurts of imperial road made of green bevelled stones. The bars – the Chinchin, the Joker. Boys throwing stones at the Muslim cemetery. Mud. A piece of sidewalk all cleaned up – to butcher a pig on. All nicely shaved and clean. It looked like me. And so, goodbye to brother pig – and you could see it knew. Join with Jack, 'for Christ's sake'.

In the church, a last supper, virgin on the roof blackened by fingers touching – like the blurs made by cat's whiskers on the whitewashed stairs. Everything playing in real time, absolutely human. A man is standing watching us, dressed in Turkish wrestler's trousers, flexing his muscles. A tall waiter with an actor's face, with deference serves us nothing. 'Why him? Why here? Why me?'

*

On the margin, yes – this is my country. Beyond those tall trees, that might be poplars decided to be willows, there lies Albania. I begin, 'The liberal mind' – and Jack's Anna catches me at once: 'For Christ's sake, Alex – not more relentless talking! Two days' relentless drive, and so mucn talk ...'

'The liberal mind,' I say, 'or one at least of its souls, invented nationalism, now doesn't know what to do with it. Here, you see, my friends, there are no liberals, and no bourgeois, or only rural ones, pettiest of petty. Albanians, like the Scots, are a people of diaspora, just like so many diasporas they have a charge of empire-builders too. So – what do we do with these awkward nationalisms we stir – that break up other, and none the less for that, obscure nationalisms? Do we sir the pot like Byron? Invitation is always a gesture whose broad sweep ends on the end – of your nose. 'If you're Irish, come into the parlour.'. But if you're not?'

'You get the hell out,' said Jack. Mysteries too deep for Jack abound.

I persevere: 'Seeking the margin is looking for what's next. The avant garde is not fermenting in the rec-rooms of Wisconsin.'

Anna says, 'I know Wisconsin well.'

Yes, well, we all know lots of countries: even the States, the evil empire that has given Jack a tic, and made Anna, hungry now and rather wolflike, smell of cinnamon. Perhaps there is such a choice of countries now, all reducible to little tradable portions, like numbered oriental dishes that we can go ape for, that we can be fans of any, making up a sporty league. For now the big battle of the angels is finished – no contest, a technical KO, or whatever unrefereed matches end in – perhaps there is just this mindless touring, looking for bits of cultures fizzling out?

The kerbstones' rosy pink holds skeins of pig blood, it's like brawn. No good, no evil; a tie that pleases everyone.

Jack's strength is being stupid, impenetrable defence: 'Jack or not Jack, one-eyed wild Jack, I have a job for you. One that requires no qualities at all, no partisanship, no discrimination between the good side and the bad side, the greens and blues, Hats and Caps, Guelphs and Ghibellines.'

Shows his teeth at me. 'Well, I just hope they stay together' – expansive gesture, to embrace the family of Yugoslav peoples.

'Come on, Jack, you of all people can't be sentimental about cohabitation. People who feel themselves oppressed set up a state that oppresses them. Every little people seeks a minority and kicks the shit out of it. Your American choice of self-determination is just racism philanthropised – up the Christians, down with the infidels. Limits of your pothead radicalism, Jack.'

More teeth. He says, 'To each his garden, Alex. The new game is self-invention. Invent a past, invent an identity. Try to forget those calls to work harder. And when you die, into the higgledy of these graveyards. Better the dogs should have your bones, Alex, than the worms.'

Some grinning dogs duly ran past, their leader sporting a mammoth shoulder-bone. Belonged to a giant ox, I hoped.

We ate in the National, a restaurant where tomorrow's sausages stood around the window and pressed their faces at us. Anna tried to flap them away. 'Anna,' I said, 'they're mules. They're bad at arguments.'

The pig had been disassembled, like a rich child's organic toy. It no longer looked like me. Jack, on the other hand, looked just like he had when he had been my friend, before he spiralled off, down into betrayal. Real betrayal, not just metaphor for times passing, times lost and sought – itches of the usual bourgeois sensibility – the only one, it seems, in store for all our lifetimes. Not just his gift for staying young, freezing at the moment when he chose his profession: betrayer, copout, cop. To lose it, who knew how, sent back to the European marches, obscurely framed in tricks and treats, but codename still betrayal. Real tricks that led to prison.

And yet, Jack had guts – so had the pig. But guts to deal with people who scared me – those of disintegration, those of integration, members of gangs, robbers, comrades of the armed party, acid freaks – he loved them all, St Francis face noble, untroubled. And the others – chiefs of police, financiers, hitmen, soldiers. Myself, I like disintegration, but it scares me, great sweep of people that I cannot love; or like. And yet, among the wretched of the earth, the dregs, of which I'm one – from universal confusion will arise not victims, not tortured angels, slaves of the word but – perhaps Jack's army.

Repels me is not confusion, but the banality, the compromise, even – and I admit – the ineffectiveness: ordinariness of hitman, unromantic nature of the good and evil drama.

I gestured around. 'This is a real collapse. Of socialism. Look at the poor people standing round: naked, unsustained.'

And Jack said, 'Well, I'm for the Serbians. When things start to crumble, choose the largest unit. Albanians! – it's just romanticism. Your head's a mare's nest, Alex.'

'It's a collapse of people, that's for sure. If it mattered, I'd be for the Albanians *and* socialism,' said Anna. I wondered 'why cinnamon', and Jack: 'Still in there fighting, my angel?'

'All they have now is being Serbian, or Montenegrin. It's being back to what you're born with. The least you can have is your parents' culture,' said Anna. Avenging angel, I wondered, or sentimental?

Jack doesn't give a damn. To him the only flag's American – love it or burn it – all the others are leaden banners carried by toy soldiers. When I knew him, before he sold his soul and started out to get a price for ours, he invented a huge musical machine. Powerful enough to blow the minds of all the other musical machines. A thrust to universalism. Jack was the inventor of the last – electric – trump. Or *an* electric trump. Never yet used, but, it would seem, a deterrent to all the others – God's included.

A talent, yes, he had – and one that broke with art as consolation. Broke your brains, broke the marble boxes. Imagination like a snake – reflected courses taken; drumming in Africa, mushrooms somewhere. An army base, perhaps. Jack was a funny man: a dreadful man. A man who would make you die, himself laughing. Yet he showed his weaknesses so large, you wanted to control him. Make Jack your instrument.

As usual he was needling Anna. But she would fight. She'd said so. And women tell the truth much more than men – I think that's true of every culture. Would fight, but still she's cold, avenging angel – carried flaming sword because she's frozen solid. If anything, she should be here with me, not Jack.

And yet – this moral charge she has: is it perhaps not just obtuse? Remarkable eye for living things, kinship with the natural and its shapes. Here in this land so earthbound, the colours waiting to fall back to dust, the houses like bits of fields, the fields like dumps of tatters, the sheep, the men, all brown like rust or dust, the cemeteries, the butchers' shops, the tarnished sunflowers – all molecules yearning to go back to bones, to mud. The lakes parched out for hydroelectricity – it seems an act of will keeps them, the molecules – together, able to communicate from zombie-land, with New York and Accra.

Yet it is that will that's drawn me here. Fascination of the great game: for me, drawing on

Jack's rope, trying to make him play his circus tricks again. To play my game, achieve my balances – and bring Jack into it! Keeping my eye on Jack, and his on me. No beating Jack – but arrange the props, and he can't resist: doing a show. The one he always does – meddling, destroying, emperor of common sense. Meanwhile, if we survive these sausages, lethal but un-pythonlike, on the end of my rope I'll make him dance!

Relentless talk will wear him down, and as he waves there in hot air, his strength will drain out, drain out into me. We'll talk, to everyone: but the stage directions will be mine.

The cars go by, now two, with furry dice and lovelights, racing tape, and Kansas jazz. Two old men, their sticks are straight, but they are bowed like ox-horns: 'Was it like this in Tirana?' asks one. 'We were not told so.' Something is moving, and can move to smother Jack, and all the other Jacks that lie behind, above him.

Anna always doing her nails. 'How long you keeping us here, Alex?'

I was angry. 'All you can see, and so all you can bother about, are people having a hard time with their budget, and taking their stand on positions that seem to you outlandish; on being proud, on hating, on being desperate, on wanting changes that you don't understand and couldn't accept if you did.

'And Jack's delighted it is all collapsing – what makes here different from London or Chicago or Hoboken. When people are forced to accept that the examples of London or Chicago are too strong for them, they never in their hearts agree to snuffle round the cold streets, at best like wage slaves and at worst like scraps of used paper.

'And then you and Jack, so keen – you on moral righteousness and Jack on pragmatism – you'll see that when Helen arrives, we two will be *contra mundum*, will be united against either one of you.'

I regretted showing my hand with such bravura. Even if it was a winning hand, some of the cards had turned themselves over or fallen on the floor as a result of my violence.

And Helen could be considerably more of a pain in the neck than Anna. But at the moment, I suppose in the way people become football fans, the idea of having something to be proud of, that was, collectively, yours, and yet did not represent anything except itself, winning or losing against similar disembodied receptacles of hope, loyalty and unrealism, fired my enthusiasm. There was too – I suppose – the mystery of speaking Albanian: my family? Friends of my family? Friends or someone, certainly, leaving a deep impression on the tongue of a little boy.

But all Anna said was, 'Watch, Jack. He's a pro. He'd eat you for breakfast if he didn't quite like you.' 'I know, I know all about Jack.'

And it would amuse him to know I covet Anna, as it would annoy him to know I intend to take her off him. Which also breaks the squared circle – meaning what to do about Helen when she arrives, secret weapon.

I said, 'Socialism in decline, is all.'

Jack said, 'Confusion, currency collapse, wars. Breakup complete.'

Anna insists: 'Alex, you must be a kamikaze – everyone wants to keep this local thing quiet and off the boil. Who wants problems in the Balkans? Jack's crowd would like to promote a quiet seethe – accent on the quiet. Your lot – your old lot – would like to cool things down. The guys here want to seethe – they've no ideas what to do afterwards. More autonomy means a faster seethe in a smaller pot – and then you dry out, inedible. And Alex – surely you've seen those beautiful polished cars, Tirana plates and all, slipping over for a chat on Sunday mornings? You and Jack want the same thing – everybody does. You bring him here, you challenge him – for what?'

'To see if I can beat him – and besides, we cannot want the same things. If we do, I've spent my time in vain. The only thing that hints of meaning is the differences between us. Struggle, conflict, complexity: what is the watch, without its parts? Jack is my enemy, not a figure in the carpet, not the next note oozing out the gramophone of time – *the enemy.*' I say it, and to me it's sense. Today, Anna smells of bubblegum, a smell that goes with larches – here, smell of burnt hoof. They hold the horses in a wooden frame, for shoeing. My grandfather held them in his hands – told me he just flipped them over, nipped them in his teeth to keep them still. A giant, my grandfather. Speaker of tongues, a muezzin, screeching out his hollow prayers, heavy and strong like iron boots or skullcaps. Told me 'I am for belief, not truth; there is one truth, and many faiths. Without the faiths – why, there's no truth: for they are the paths, the ways that lead – or may not lead – up to that central point, that truth.'

Sixty years, old granddad, and that centre's gone, paths crisscrossed until they make an agora, earth and grass all beaten down, and merchants selling things.

*

Talk to Milo, face and suit of boss, who says one bright thing – 'If you know the battle's over, then you know you've lost' – but then is drunk with fancy. 'Take ourselves off to Germany. We Slavs from the

South were destined there – somewhere about Dortmund, even, perhaps, the Rhine. All in a line, from Aix to Moscow, centres of Slav power. Our genius' (his face shines like the sun) 'is not down here, among the Southerners, the logic choppers, it lies in the grand design, the Northern purpose. And a life *indoors*.'

I ask, 'And the honest burghers, where shall they go, the Germans?' Has it figured out. I've heard the same in diners, bars of the diaspora, my united states I've never seen.

'They'll go where their destiny, their star was leading. Lapland, with its forests and its cold. Estonia, with its famous endive, its kohlrabi, its little beans as pure and sweet as pearls ...' And a sea as thick as soup, and fogs as salt as seas, its church towers sharp as minarets, and in the forests, bears who cobble, maidens who live a thousand years, resisting penetration … by the postman, through the letterbox, while Mutti steams the stamps off, changes the address – so no one gets my daughter, just the boy next door. Who's taken off, it seems, off in a sealed train to see the ice queen, her lips still bloody, cheeks as red, red as a candy-apple, or a matrioshka full, we can guess, of disturbing, even alarming, upsurges.

Jack said, Can't wait, can't wait, to shake this peasant Europe off my boots, out my beard, out my nose ...'

'No, Jack,' I said. 'I need you here. Besides, what will they leave us, what do they mean to us, the marches, the margins of our continent?'

'To you,' said Jack rudely, 'they should mean nothing. You don't want roots, you want seven league boots. You wanted to shovel these horse thieves and onion planters under some sterile sod somewhere. You commie bastards are all the same,' (he showed his teeth, a genuine laugh this time), 'Everyone into the towns, you said, everyone into the technical institutes. Instead – everyone in line outside the salami shop, hopes of a peek at the porno video. Big problem for you – little problem for me. Welcome back to the human race, Alex. And then you whinge – Jack, Jack, nasty Jack – there must be something more. Yes, Alex, there is. Lots more, whatever you want. And then you die. But you die to nice clean music in the hospice, not to the red ants chomping you up by the Amazon, or turning back into shit in Calcutta.'

Anna said, 'Isn't that a bit brutal and flip, Jack?' she was smelling of cinnamon again, and I felt the tension between the wind from the shore, sprinkled with cinnamon, and the wind from the sea, the waves pushed slowly on like clouds. Jack says,

'Yes, but Alex only responds to extremes – above the waist he's a romantic, and below, he's sentimental. The democratic male works the other way round. Alex was put together wrong. As for me, he can die where he likes – so long as he doesn't make everyone else ascend the pyre.'

'But Jack,' says Anna, 'you speak as if you're the supreme product of everyone else's aspirations – and as if you've *made* them produce you, or else. I don't expect humility and respect, but perhaps some cautious perspective?'

But I know Jack is needled, that he's accepted my challenge. Or a situation he finds challenging. He is doing what he has to do, being what he has to be. We are the two last men of our world, professionals of confrontation, two fallen or falling angels, standing firmly on the points of our needles – or perhaps there was one for both of us – at all events, a truly Olympic feat. Mars and Apollo.

Mars, with age, cannot walk with all his armour on. Apollo can still hitch up the chariot of the sun, outspanned somewhere behind the Rattlesnake Diner in Nevada, where the real sunsets used to be – but everyone knows ... the sun no longer goes round the earth.

'Our gods are fallen angels,' I say out loud, and Anna jumps and drops her baklava. Now, she only eats cakes. She is becoming fat and irritable. I think, 'A spy's moll. An agent's cover.'

I say, 'Why Jack, why him? Surely you know about the Mexico Olympics? Of course you do.'

'Yes,' she says, 'Jack did not behave well. Behaved badly, in fact. Unforgivably. But then – I'm not in the forgiving business. He's a very sensitive person, man, to me, I mean.'

Jack had promised protection, refuge to some students – and instead reneged, the kindest said, but most agreed, he'd lured them to a beating from the cops, causing death, vegetation – both.

I am still puzzled, after all these years; it's a real scar you can't read any way at all, except that it really happened, caused real pain. No re-reading, no faults of one's own. He, in every sense an agent, responsible, and not for any more pressing or more sententious truth. And yet he certainly retains all the signs of being in his, in her eyes, an exceptional, even dominant person. Who talks of love and death, the limits of acceptable power, and unacceptable gender-typing. He is inspired by courage, loves – so he has us think – the strength of simple materials. If it were necessary he'd introduce Ravel, and the pussycat, to North America. In short, a poet of the everyday, and even something more.

'I must go talk to some monks,' Jack had said that morning. We heard he had been amused by his spiritual quest. A monk, deeply into German soft porn, had quizzed him on the air-fares to Dublin. 'They are awful sectarians here', he told Jack. 'They even argue over whether to plant radishes. Myself, I like them. But our salaries are so low. The Adventists do much better – they even get dollars.' So, while Jack enjoyed himself, I had had Anna to myself, my 'Why Jack,' and her 'Why not? Why does it bother you so much?'

Off every bridge in this country, the Germans hanged as many as they could. 'And there were,' said Jack, 'the Cominconformists – not too soft a ride.' I mentioned this to Anna – again. She says, don't have the moral stature, don't have the language. 'And when you two use these bodies – not out of pity, nor yet quite indifference – but to fight your battles with – then I'm appalled. I see you as two ghouls fighting with bones in graveyards. And for that, I value Jack's simplicity. He has no idea what he makes happen, he's a cripple on the moral plane, but we must all be. His ignorance saves him.'

I said, 'But if you reduce these things to symmetries, it all comes back to literature, to effect. Jack's ignorance you value as simplicity, as if to say: the weakness of his brain is compensated by his long arms. You just do publicity: pity and terror are, for the moment, out. The easy moralism palls. Fascism – is just a transgression against the word. But then – today's word *is* transgression. And you, Anna, don't condone, but you won't punish either. You renounce a vengeance, because, in the last resort, we are all to blame. So – superiority on the moral plane is won, by you, in quiet indifference to the terrible.'

And Anna says, 'Alex, what *you* say is rhetoric – you're an open book, you should be closed, trapped in it, like a witch in the wood. We must find a new way of living, not based on forgiveness but on – perhaps – indifference. Even we must love those incapable of loving without violence, accept for them the bullying that they don't recognise, that they can't accept, that lies within them ...'

I said, 'And gives meaning to everything they are. Or, since I'm clearly one of them – being human in a world that's made only of Jacks and Alexes, with here and there a fragrant furry Anna gentling us along – you make us minor characters in a bigger text, a subplot to a story which is invented by a more alert, a more refined intelligence. And so, these perverted goblins who share your bed and hound you, are just creatures from some invention – which can wound and tear but somehow – is not the real story, the real unravelling of what there, after all, must be ...'

'Yes, Alex: it's your reality that must be lowered, by my fantasy, my imagination.'

Of which, I thought disgruntled, there is much talk and much display, but little evidence. An age of contemplation? Well, I'm a collector, displayer, scene-shifter. If not making things, then moving them around – showing thereby respect for other makers and arrangers. What it all does, what it all means – is sometimes less than clear. At times, all this activism, this discrimination – or lack of it – just seems bad for the liver. No picture of anything, no penetration of surfaces. Flight of eagle, five minutes before the sunset, always in blood-red light, but below – no features. A few silver roads, perhaps, diagonal striped over deserts, a dam broken here, holding there. But catastrophes subsumed, all taken in their stride by that speeding arc of darkness. the sunset driving on the bird, so fast, we think it's eagle. Could as easily be a vulture, though.

At all events, the bird's omnivorous, but Anna – prophet on her rock. Yet knowing only rock, the baby fish, some bellying up, the miniature pink carnations and all around carnelian rock, sea the colour of the tough green of roads Philip of Macedon might have started. In the old days she would have sat, alone in her village, listening to the priest, as lonely as a single cat yet knowing through her ears and whiskers what all the other cats know, all that it's useful for a cat to know. To me – eternally passive, seeing it all, retiring into type. Not consuming, suffering, maintaining. Calling it love, calling it faith, calling it imagination. Or just a catlike modesty, that can't do any different.

'Well, here we are' – three centuries, me the nineteenth, Jack is ours, and Anna the perpetual new year, coming on us with a hangover and a diary blank.

Iniquities. Coming under fire – in Rome. For me, the first time, a demo, people firing, some with blanks. All there in uniform – final resolution of the papal punishments: a whipping for eating wrong food on fast days, veal guts, cow's teat, perhaps; or rudeness to the wife of the community cop. Now, for real, the last transgression, laying the dust of Artisan City, republican fervours. And now – here's Anna to sort it out. Bury those mounds of dead, dishonour those classical battlements, mix up the orders, untune the guitars, take the full-stops out of the printers' founts – even spin long ropes of genes, confusing the cells, fiddling our handicaps, making anger derisory, breaking the continuities, memory. Not at all bad. not a bad thing, but also, in its mad way, rather ambitious, rather close, perhaps to the concerns Anna would rather skate across?

Using the ruins of a ruined world to build – more ruins, covered with scarlet foxgloves: except the world's not ruined – least of all where we talk of ruins most.

And Helen will come, to help to head Jack away – Helen, who understands so well the eroticism of the mind. Anna is like those German girls – made purer, healthier, in the East. Responding to the challenges, glad to be made orphans, and then must strive, must strive, strive not to see the granddads and the parents, widows and brothers: who have taken socialism as their husband, as their blood – immense transfusions. Meetings where the clock is at your shoulders, only the speaker knows when he's had enough. And then, bursting out – after so many years it seems – laughing, and speechless, yes, fired up with words but running through the gardens, breaking off the boughs of blossoms that should bring fresh pears and apples in the fall. Big trouble there.

Helen came from the South, from Greece, to join us in our 'situation'. She's a good foil: controls my trend to covet things and people – like Anna; and cook up situations so complex they fall like honeycombs whose architect forgets rule number one – simple uniformity. She said, 'Well, things don't fall apart at the edges, at the seams. This is a margin, a march, if you prefer, holds together nothing but itself, holds no one out – and so,' to me, 'why get so excited?'

'To some of us,' I say, 'this was the alternative to the alternative. I want to keep the big guys out. Or at least let the little players have their game, their fun.'

'And their illusions, and your fun. Alex, what is happening here has gone on happening, like original sin. It's a slide area, a shadow zone. At best it's on the way between some choicer areas, and at worst, it passes from some poor, slack pasha to someone tough, who'd like to see it all reduced and asphalted over.'

We have the opposite faults, that she believes just nothing, and I everything. I want to make a story – she's paid to, and out they come. As with Anna, my invented nature for her doesn't fit. But Anna likes to talk about it, why men who think can think that way, what can be done about it. Helen, on the other hand, just doesn't care. She knows it, so she isn't curious. The problematic bits don't interest at all – problem for me but not for her.

She'd just done a story 'How Brazil feeds her neighbours' – with contraband, that is. Now she said, 'Alex, you think other people lack rigour, power to balance contradictions on their noses. Really, you are quite incoherent – you want everything – order and wealth, autonomy and flute playing. Perhaps you're right – you can have all together, beefsteaks and icecream. But you may also have to choose. Sometimes in choosing you must do without icecream for years. Sometimes, more or less innocently, you condemn the icecream men to poverty. Certainly, quite consciously, you condemn the cows to die. Perhaps we can, we should, contrive to live on icecream. But insisting on both means you vomit. I don't care if you vomit, or if Bolivians have Mercedes. But, Alex' – we sat down to our sausages – 'you do seem to have made an awful mess. The best you can say is – well, it's not so bad as some others. But if that's rigour ... Steak and icecream is fantasy, Alex, dream of a little boy, just stick to writing it down, making us long for it – for being little boys. I speak as a little girl ...'

Imagination stuck in the countryside? Perhaps, but Helen isn't wanted to expand my mind, but to help me in my fight with Jack. Icecream. Beefsteaks. Imagine!

After ten minutes, Helen said, 'I know all I want about this place,' though someone was telling us, 'And I'd like to go back to Turkey. When grandfather was there we had a hotel. And then they threw us out. But it's all changed now' – he desperately wanted to say the manager of the wood factory should have been his uncle.

'You see,' I told Helen, 'where there is one dislodgement after another, people do make simple comparisons.'

'All right,' she said. 'Then being stuck here is worse than being massacred. Even in LA one doesn't feel the fire and sword are waiting round the corner – though perhaps they are. But then there's the filip to the brain given by technology and the sciences – a jolt that opens the mind's door ...'

'I trained as an electronics man,' said the cakeseller. 'Electronics is one of the older sciences,' I said, 'and now démodé. What binds the tongue and brain together, that is all the rage these days.'

'Relentlessly talking, Alex,' said Helen. 'You've got us mustered here, Anna the avenging angel, Jack the simple agent, and me – I suppose – the recording angel.'

'Well,' I said, 'you are at least a witness.'

'But you, Alex, who are you? Who are you?' she asked.

'I'm the one who tells you to move on, which we must.'

Sometimes, we seem Martians, dumped down by numbers, stamped out like brass biscuits, fluent but tongueless.

*

Moving North over this immense stubbly plain, a sprawling dusty chin taking the blows from two armies of people, Turks and Serbs, the splinters – still in the form of people, still lying round – of teeth, of bone, impacted whiskers. A city made of Lego blocks, steam coming from the top – colours of a Fifties childhood –

red oxide, blue-green and mustard. Trailing off in the foreground into shacks, the housing list no longer buried in the barrios but springing to the visitor's eye. Of course – in slums here there is more room, a lower density: under the shaggy, grown-out poplars, jigging around all day on donkeys, feet sticking out like the handles of a wheelbarrow.

'This must be a via dolorosa for you, Alex,' said Jack.

'I suppose it is.'

'If this were the States,' Helen went on, 'they'd be organised in gangs or romanticised by social workers – or both.'

'And here they're just poor. Or last in line. Or both. It's better without romanticism, don't you think, Jack?' I said.

Jack persisted, 'You and your fat friends might do something about it, though, Alex. Or about the gypsies – never used to be a problem, now they're a misery to themselves and everyone else – I hear the locals shoot their dogs.'

Certainly these chains start far back, vendettas and blood feuds survive and grow, bound in a chain of rationalisation and shame, protection, appeals to the past. But on whose neck do we wield the axe? Not, this time, on Jack's, but then ... Perhaps on the weakness of the centre, weakening its peripheries, finding quite new people to drop in its dirt. Or else – while one thinks – where would moralism be without the poor, where would talk of human diversity, the species' unbreakable spirit be?

'I've never heard such an unedifying conversation,' said Anna. 'If you're both the real politicians, without constituencies and who can really do what you think the rest of us would – if there were no checks on us – then we are all gone to the end of the world! You represent fag-ends of cultures. You are the intelligent edge of the middle voice you say you despise.'

Indeed, rolling along in our motor-car, we looked stylised, a mobile coin-type, a vignette from the Thirties. The living were the people who had hoped our hum was to be their bus, or trudging along had given up hopes of rides from us. I said, 'Perhaps we should acquire a sense of place. And yet Jack had one, it seemed – at least in the bars in Titograd. And a sense of identity – but Helen too should have one of those – or at least of judgement, internationally circulated.'

Jack had been fermenting Anna's remarks. 'Well, Anna, to represent middle opinion is surely what we want, guaranteeing our plausibility – and our careers. Almost everyone believes their special messiah has already been and left his – and now I must say her – message. We have made – we are – our trap.

Accepting death, we have learned to love, accept, our bodies. Even old Alex's Marx was looking for a way out – relentless criticism; of everything that exists. Relentless talk. Now, we accept our lot. We're indefinitely limited. Loved or ignored by all our gods – and, indeed, we are unlovable, ignorable. We accept our calling – to the bar of cosmic indifference. What's left is to explore the cage, twangle on the pipes, peer through the keyhole, speculate about the other cells a million light-years away. A delicate operation, requiring not the equality, the comradeship of all the prisoners, but a process of fierce selection. Our poor cakeman couldn't make the cut. Didn't understand the physics of the mousetrap, the astrophysics of the cage. The only thing for him is baklava.

'While we go on, perhaps to blow our minds: finding on that last star the magic mushroom. Waiting to be picked, marinated, distilled and sniffed. One last, heart-stopping revelation. Then the other guys will start again to tap tap tap the walls.'

Defile. Nature severely manipulated here. Water levels fallen back. High-stepping Macedonian tortoise, shell pulled down like Alexander's helmet, dancing on unlikely toes. Trucks always uphill, panting survivors in carpet slippers: shuffle and pant. Forests carefully logged by horse, cosmetic snipping, even here and there a thankful wolf. Then swooping down, descent somehow a success, old Soviet film-end, into the little town. Brown water rushing under the streets, puddling out along the river-bed. Minarets on their launching pads, churches stacked with benches so tight no one could sit down. Popes and their popelets affable in the street – it could be Cork. but there are imams too.

The dance to get us rooms occludes all thought of sex, solution of three rooms between four gives it an Ottoman ring, perhaps we are some literary quartet, although – I fear – the style must be against us.

I hear Jack say to Anna, 'Alex knows everyone, on both, on all, the sides. Another season, dry season, here and I'll have earned my spell back in the States.' She doesn't speak. Occurs to me, that it's not her I want at all. Perhaps it's her silences I want, though they're filled, I must admit, with my own speculations. Not the appetite, the full stomach: neither thirst nor hangover, but being, like the watchman, full.

Helen too – how can a woman wear a suit here, with a skirt? When she sees those sour apple-greens, those violets with a silver thread, and always the red and black – girls with red scarves and Turkish faces or perhaps from an evening country, province of the night, Sheherazade: indeed, from Shiraz ... is it absurd that seeing them, I should think 'they're free'? – a delusion, sure, but at least they look happy.

Helen, instead, lives at the limit of the freedom quest for knowledge gives. Not happy, certainly, and she knows that being smart, in clothes and mind, brings no freedom she can recognise. And she's right. The stereotypes run on, though we speak of breaking with traditions, roots, we see them all around, we think these are backward who have five or six hundred years of unresolved conflicts, culture clash, and yet all we have done is become disillusioned with what isn't at least two thousand years or more. It's true, the bones so old weigh less, shine, like radium skeletons. Looking up our human forbears, overlaid with beasts in from the forest, or Wisconsin.

The watchman's bar's still closed. Sign has raised no eyebrow. Perhaps what I mean by freedom is really powerlessness. If you have no power, you have no guilt, so you do not suppress your memory. And if you don't suppress your memories, perhaps you are free to have emotions? Like I and Jack and Helen don't have – or have them just to order, on the right occasions for our characters.

The building the watchman guarded still finishes at its knees. Why put the windows in, when they'd soon be smashed – or even put in smashed, to show they were delivered right? No watchman now, best way to guard a padlocked site – lose the key. So be it.

We four are all mixed up – no longer differentiated by class, or our ideas – and yet it is these shades that shape response and conflict. Colours, perhaps, washed out, like a sky that's watered down to make a smooth path for planes (and perhaps for minarets that burn out on re-entry, like mosquitoes on the grill). A girl is singing – I am still half in thoughts about Shiraz.

I say, 'You've a fantastic voice.' Rare, I'd say quite absent here, a girl with an instrument, to play alone. Yet here, to sing alone but as though there was a public out there – you, practising your music while they appropriate you, your sex, your body – that's not unusual, but the intensity is.

'I'm studying,' she says. Wears a violet scarf, with little silver ropes across it, harness of a twilight sea. I feel it then, flute in the desert, lifting the blind in the gritty sleeping train and seeing Babylon.

'And I collect,' I said. And it could as well be true.

Betu, her name – I don't ask why. Perhaps we're cousins, even kissing ones.

We talk a little about schools and conservatories. She has a great dark sack full of secrets she wants to dump at my feet. I am the stranger, but also bear the passkey – shared language, even if I don't understand too well.

'Are you afraid?' I ask.

'No, why ever should I be?' She puts the pieces of the puzzle together, not noticing that they don't fit – 'I am a citizen. This is my home.'

'But', I push relentlessly on, 'your music doesn't recognise the two. Citizen and home.'

That was the problem: 'home' was a way of singing, studying: and a public. Perhaps she'll make it to the watchman's bar. She doesn't want to talk about it. 'Yes, they were the best. But hard for me to go there – so much drinking! Not in our tradition, that is, I mean, our interests. So much trouble comes from drink. By evening tempers are short.' She is so fluent, so uncertain.

But,' she says, 'citizenship means singing other peoples' songs', or rather, 'It means lieder, opera. Perhaps even an international circuit. It's a terrible problem, and involves my whole family.'

'But,' I ask, 'the politics.'

'Yes,' says Betu, 'it's natural we want to be free, responsible. As things are, we're quite poor, and to add to this – there are some terrible prejudices ... The little ones at school – the mothers come to take them home, and they are kept apart.'

Well, then, and on to music, that funny language, with an effort we can understand it anywhere in the world – and yet it always says different things. Or to us, citizens of the world, often nothing at all. Or perhaps things untranslatable.

Behind the fence of Betu's house, there is her courtyard, and her family, animals in various degrees of kin and friendship.

What life here, after the formal mingling of the street. Shows what homeland means. Long and inconclusive discussion of musical styles. The older ones want the conservatory and prestige, objectify the situation but not her; perhaps want her to give it up and choose them instead. Others estimate the life-chances, the hybrid pop on tapes that go the rounds. The old ones know the birds will never sing their songs again, the new bird never learns the same.

What is drawing her? Calculations of technique and style – but she also sits there waiting to be chosen – going North, never a simple choice. A boyfriend, 'Red', strains at a clarinet, will never make it: my rival, my brother – my cousin, at least – eyes popping out, cheeks like a pottery jug.

'And then there's Red,' she says and sighs. For her, with me, a safe flirtation – for me, instead, I see the water pulling me down.

I am an other, and I see her calling to me, like the man who followed the gypsy girl when he went to cut a new pin for his axle in the forest. Talk of 'communicating things' – but what things does she have except herself?

When she has reconciled the claims of her uncles, she will still be elegantly trapped, but in her vocal chords. I have deserted Helen – I imagine her speaking of patriarchies, she too imprisoned by the 'piece' she's writing, tongueless, about the local scene. Jack is back to the bars, waiting for me, waiting for whatever move I make, 'his job' to keep an eye on me, since I know everyone here, can promise the aid of armies vast, peoples combative, or less so – but at least a score of fingers to stick in this particular pie.

Betu's family wear their modernity lightly – perhaps indeed for them it doesn't wear so heavy. They watch on the TV a Protestant ethic at grips with ruffians in the woods of Oregon – justice is done with many subtitles. In Betu I see not just my youth, lived over and better, but ever new chances of being foolish, love her like a mirror, selective mirror that reflects only what I want to see.

'I can't see you in the cafe, fattish, dare I say flamboyant, even if the best.'

She said, 'They have the best there is. And I'd have a watchman to look after me.'

'We all need one of those,' I said. 'Do they come over the borders – the singers – the songs?'

Behind every flirtation there is more than innocence, perhaps, a deeper innocence.

'The border is closed,' she says, dreamily, as if to a child. With her uncles, I am back in the old days – the Italians, the carnival queens, the French expedition, loyalty and the king. Politics of a kind that Jack would understand – or at least feel at home in using.

Besides all this, there is the problem of Red – who's not even a rival, just a kid. Quite big, quite bright, quite forceful, even. My privilege is having her report everything he says – but though this too is part of the flirtation, it's the part that is delivered with indifference; if things mattered more, I suspect it would be done to hurt, to spur.

'Well anyway,' she says. 'You've got two women and a big loping shadow. How many times are they going to see the churches. And how long will you stay? They're not your people – not our people. Helen's very ambitious, isn't she? I wouldn't think you'd do for her. Nor, of course, that she would do for you. But Anna's pretty – and she doesn't look down her nose at things – you know, we have a lot to do here – and your friend Jack, he's such a bully, such a tease.'

They had wolfed her down, the only palatable thing I'd brought them. Source of carefully prepared, but not inaccurate, remarks on everything. But everything! Who was in town, what the boys herding goats in the riverbed wanted to be, whose pension didn't stretch, how much were grapes. Everything. Helen wrote it down, Jack teased Betu and remembered everything, Anna was bored. And I was bored.

Red was a difficulty. Perhaps Betu made him one – a difficulty – for himself, for herself. She said, 'He acts so old, so domineering – yet he seems to want a relation out of an old book.'

'Identity problem. Role crisis,' I explained, with satisfaction.

'No, Alex, it's not that he doesn't know how to act, He doesn't want to know me.'

'Perhaps he's working towards homosexuality' I suggested.

'Yes, that's it exactly!' I'd hit the target, back turned, eyes closed, from another room. 'Yes,' she said, and I felt that then, perhaps, she loved me, loved my guess, my intuition, or else she didn't see me as a courtesan, gathering around people that I couldn't satisfy – had no wish or intention to satisfy, let into that secret space that I for one knew had been so often isolated. Surely everyone knew. It was true. I collected people. Didn't know what to do with them. But it was a beginning, perhaps an alternative, to other things, a deeper exchange. For what purposes, perhaps one didn't know.

*

Anna was having language problems. First the eating, now a tedious abstinence – though still, I noticed, based on cakes.

'I can't speak,' she would complain as we had to order for her, thus reduced to tourist package.

Mostly, they discussed me. Jack said, 'Alex is in shock over what's happened in Russia. Sees it all breaking up,' said with his usual satisfaction.

'Well, it is,' said Helen. 'Will affect us all, and not just spies and academics, Jack. Not that you'll be without work, but when the ice breaks up – it's an impressive but a dangerous thing. We think we're standing on the shore, but it may well be we're on a little shard of ice, twirling away, faster and faster in the spate. Alex has already found how small his cold block of security was – the fact he called it principles, frigid though they were, just makes his position worse.' So, sympathy from Helen, even, one would say, an understanding. Spies, academics and journalists might have made a better trio, though.

My time with Betu was not only guileless, being beguiled. Somewhere inside, there was my Russian soul, self-exile. And this – incongruously, for Betu had the spirit of the pastoral, the unmediated life of the uplands, even though she lived on a plain and on a rickety urban street – gave a depth, synthetic meaning, to our walking out. Talking about Red, bless him, about the trees that needed lopping, and were we ready, able to meet the new challenges, or was it perhaps a return to normality, to before the war ...

'Yes, yes,' says Betu, and adds, 'If necessary.'

I tell her, 'But it won't be like that. It never was. It's another dream. At least we were accused so often of being dreamers, we knew the difference between what we hoped, and screaming nightmares. And yet, you see – when you're faced with a choice – supremely traditional, I may say – between the music of the folk and music of the people – you can't decide.'

'Well, then,' she argues, 'perhaps it's not an important choice, perhaps it matters just to me.'

'It could be that, but at home it generates a lot of heat,' I say – and think of Jack, reduced to lecturettes on Bo Diddley.

Here, not the high noon of the Russian novel, partridges in the hedge, the sons perhaps in Norfolk jackets or even with horns and huntsmen in the tapestry forests: serfs with their wooden business on the edge. Nor yet these same fields – hedgeless now – when the combines come, the men blue-eyed – we read – driving their hungry steeds, courtesy of the MTS. No, here the serfs have gone – so too the tractors. Look like ragpickers harvesting the stones (with here and there, I see, some crumbs of marble, green and pink). 'The demonstrations here,' I say to Betu, 'are like nothing I've ever seen. Not like the modern world at all, with guns and desperation. It's like the last century, you're right. But also ugly things are said, the others' – I mean the Serbians – 'bear a strong charge of exasperation – not to put it stronger.' It's clear that I don't understand, and not just here.

'Perhaps you've lost conviction, or assurance, Alex. Perhaps you need adventure.'

Helen is writing her piece. Honest, sensitive, superficial and dull.

Anna exasperates Jack, as she must. She mustn't chase him off, as they perhaps would both prefer.

'You're not interested in my voice,' says Betu.

'I'm more interested in you,' I tell her. Perhaps the time has come.

She understands why we are all interested in coming here – but thinks our interest lies in something intrinsic to her, her friends, her people. That gives her confidence, and value, and I guess it doesn't wholly matter that on our part it's false. A professional lie.

'You must realise, Betu,' I say, 'that while we are all – on a global scale – becoming friends, not everyone is equally welcome. The need for order may exclude you. Also, you're poor, which doesn't help.

Self-confident, which perhaps is worse. And then, you're in the middle ...' I was almost saying between the real Albanians and the rest, but she said, 'Yes, we're the diaspora – but you should understand.'

'I do, but that's not necessarily an advantage.'

Prayers were announced. 'Is that a real muezzin, or a tape?' I asked.

'All the muezzin are real,' she said impatiently.

I crash onward: 'I want to avoid, with all this friendship, a solution that is too friendly, that is, too drastic, a solution being imposed. Money to some, to others tolerance and prestige. The troubled sea is calmed – and comes the *pax romana*, perfect, if not eternal, peace. I don't want other people to achieve their ends at your expense. Even if their ends are laudable.'

'You're very slick, Alex,' she says.

Slick? It's probable, but surely, not just now. I want the pot to bubble. But on what principle? I like bubbles and I like pots. There must be something more complicated, slicker than that.

'Don't get Jack wrong,' I add. 'Jack's a professsional. You tell him to be intelligent, he will be – sensitive, the same. It's just that by his nature he's pretty much a philistine, pretty cloddish. Lives in Europe as if it was a foreign language he'd learned well in Texas. At home, but – like his home – not where he wants to be.'

'In that case,' Betu asks, 'what slot do you have for me? Helen, for instance: she's aware that things are complex, so is sympathetic to all sides. But then she has to dominate them all. Anna wants to get close to things, but people have to like you for that to happen – she's afraid that they won't like her, and often enough she's right – she's very – plastic, isn't she?'

'You're not bad at this. I confess I'm disappointed. I thought you were more ingenuous.'

What a marvel for self-sacrifice I am. This place, the feeling of everyone on the move, or caravans, obsessive, insecure, just driving on from one donkey camp to the next: shops where you get a shave, a green tea. What do the imams find to talk about? Of course, most people have settled down: or live on letters home from those who've left.

'I appreciate you wanting us to be left alone,' says Betu, 'but what are we supposed to do? Being left alone is rather like being left in a corner while everyone else does the interesting things.'

'Well, yes,' I agree. 'That is the weakness of my position – there's rather a vacuum of ideas, and power. I wouldn't like to live in your uncles' backyard.' Not a tactful thing, since she will have to live in their yard till she finds a more decisive Lochinvar than Red.

I try again: 'When it comes to loosening the centres of power, other powers supervene. You, here, are on the edge, so you are the most vulnerable. All you have is each other – and the new ways represent the opposite of this.'

What can I say. 'I want to help you sing like a bird. And so, you must help me against Jack. No more than that.'

In fact, my 'Russian soul' tells me it is rather little. My own soul tells me I'm losing my chance with Betu. Chance of what? We never know. In this case, absurd and complicated things, which drag us along all the same. Desire for warmth, a simple cause, a watchman who's your friend. Things always hard to find, and with the years, a rusty old irony takes hold.

*

'I have loved you,' said Betu as I went back to the hotel, 'But it could have been better.'

*

The others, in their turn, had plotted during my absence. Helen was prickly, Anna curious – my plans for her I'd ostentatiously put on ice while I was angling Betu. Jack affected to be amused, talked of my 'conspiracy in a minor key', but was curious enough as well to see how I would exercise my arid powers, spinning my webs, putting dessicated flies in my larder.

Clearly they had planned to take the initiative, a campaign permitting more mobility, less dependence on the cafes where the idle came to discuss with them plans for new dislocations of the people, revolutions and reforms.

That evening, as I had anticipated, we were all imprisoned.

Prison, I pointed out, was more spacious than the car we had travelled in, less expensive and quieter than the hotel. Indeed, Anna said, when we had smoothed our feathers and mastered our first feelings of panic, 'Alex is in his element. Safe and a victim at the same time.'

Jack, I must admit, was exemplary: he did everything middle America did on this occasion. He even shook the door to check the lock held. Then he showed his teeth – 'It's a great scenario – but who's out there in the audience?'

After a long time a dish of peppers was brought, the first vegetables we had been close to eating for some weeks. 'Are they hallucinogenic?' I asked.

'If a leaf-green aardvark should pass ...' said Jack.

But the peppers left us where they found us. The world went on outside, and even inside – as the wheels of a watch must feel as they rub together and grind out a flowing record of a different and – to them – invisible time.

'The travellers should tell a story,' I said. 'Since there's no telephone, we must amuse each other. *Lex dura, sed lex*.'

Jack says: 'Alex, I'm very cross with you. You've muddled us in here. We were observers, and you've been fiddling with the locals, fanning the flames, who knows. Inflaming the local cops, who are what they are, and know your first principle is stirring things up. Second principles – socialism, autonomy, popular culture, nostalgia for the birch trees and the cherry orchards, one sweet and one sour? Start to recognise yourself? No, it's you and only you who are responsible.'

'Leave me here. Tell them what you say and rat out. Me in jail, you in the hotel covering my story. Nice.'

Wistfully from Anna. 'Jack, we can't leave him I suppose.' Jack is silent. Anna goes on,

'We can't leave him. And we can't get out either. There seems to be no jailer, watchman, guard. Besides, prisons are structured. They don't leave you alone. This isn't structured,' says Helen.

'Well,' Jack decides, 'I'll tell you a story, but not a pleasant one, because I don't feel pleasant. I was by a lakeside. Something was not quite consistent. Looking down the inconsequential patterns of granite cobbles, past the fishermen's houses – less machines for living in than burrows – to where, perhaps, the sunset was just beginning over the water ... over the dark green mountains, shaped almost regularly like mounds of poured green marble dust, towards the mane of hills and sulphur mines – mane now like a lizard's, where the sun would soon set like a division of scarlet banners. Scarlet banners all cut from the same field of cloth, and behind them the gold lacquer on leather armour. Cracking and fading off till the lizard brown of the mountains and their yellow sulphur scars, the copper-gold of the armour, turned into the same brown, reflected brown in the sky, and the banners went down like an army drowned in its ranks without a word. Gone under the lake water with lips clamped, not a chink for the eels to get in and clean them out. Army, in the end, unarmed.

'There were four of us, taking a vacation, designing a kind of water-sled. Just fooling about, just playing about with shapes and propulsions.

'The locals weren't too keen. Said it was a rocket, threat to the fish, threat to the sea monsters, threat to their peace, their women – you all know the score. But for us – all quite innocent and clean.

'And so, when we decided it was time to leave – and not wanting to take away our Rosebud, as we called it, we decided to leave it, with a message and a joke to all who'd given us a hard time there.

'We towed the sled out to the middle of the lake.

'We bought the carcasses of four old sheep. We sat them in the seats. We left them there, dressed lightly in our clothes – as though we'd been transmogrified into little old ladies struck down on a summer outing.

'What would the people think? At worst, a kind of insult, at the best, that there had been a sea change, and a challenge, that we hadn't really left by early taxi, but had been transformed.'

Jack was shaken with remembered laughter, and renewed delight.

'What a foul story,' said Helen.

'I'm not an aristocrat like Jack,' she continues. 'Nor am I a populist like Alex. When I see people here who call for pashas, others who call to Ataturk, I feel something is wrong. Populism right or left, striding along, or congealing into prisons of various sorts. If it must be that, then I must say – "The people – no", or less provocatively, "You, the people dispose, but I shall continue to propose." And for that, must always be outside, seeking the company of my peers in telex rooms, hotel lobbies, libraries, the antechamber. But at least I shall avoid the craziness of Alex's outsider – now meddling with the grand design, now tramping along for a few leagues with the blaspheming legionaries.

'Here is my cautionary tale. Also against myself. It was in the States, and a young black Muslim was accused of torching a store. As usual I was doing a piece – but not in the city, this was over the edge. This guy had torched the only store in some village, and the people there would have roasted him three times over, for what he claimed to be, for what they said he'd done.

'His father made an interesting play. A very devout man, a minister. He begged to take his son's place – first because the law required, for punishment, responsibility – and this his son quite clearly didn't have; everyone was agreed on that. And then because the other, the son, had put himself outside the culture, had linked conscience to race, and criminality to religion. In this sense, this liberal sense, his son could not be punished because he was outside the code. The community should recognise the father as the only moral person who could be punished – even if the act itself had been committed – as it were – by a being from another planet, a stranger working under other laws, related to quite different, inhuman myths.

'In fact, the judge said, "We cannot try dissent, or one who has put conscience outside our reach." Of course, the father would have felt, perhaps earned, guilt by association. Hard, though, to see his blame as anything except generic. But certainly it made a point: to the moralists who wanted to see someone suffer – fully aware: and to many, too, who preferred a Christian black to suffer for his son, rather than some smartass telling them about their racism.

'And so it was, and so it came about. The father took the son's place, and dangled in the breeze, was mocked, probed by psychiatrists, fingerprinted, stripped of his flock – became a case of guilt for which a crime and punishment must be invented. For us – a story that seemed at once to justify our liberal minds, and to show up their dialectic.

'There was, alas, a snag, which did collapse the plot of all who seemed to benefit, all living intensely and being justified. The old pastor hadn't realised that at that time all black Muslims took new names that sounded – in that case it might be exactly – like the one his son had taken. In short, it wasn't his son. He never showed – underground, or dead or jailed, we never knew?

'The relationship doesn't seem to me to matter,' said Anna.

'It did to him. And me,' said Helen. 'Without some relationship, we are all guilty of everything and nothing, nothing is specific, and so the specific holds absolute sway.'

To me, Helen's story seemed quite dodgy, if not bogus, but I must confess my own apparatus doesn't let me comment. If you don't believe in Helen's standards, and I suspect her hierarchies, her story is really rather funny. Not that my sentimental chums would agree, but, told properly, it's a hoot.

'To me,' Anna starts off, 'you have got it wrong. What is a story in a jail? It is something that helps you get out. Preferably physically, if not, then morally. So when Helen says "a prison is structured", you can add "a prison is structured like a story", but also "a prison, like a story, may be opened with a key". So my story is about that key.

'When I was young, I was a golden girl, a golden little girl. Too good to be true, but real all the same. Everyone knew it had to end – but how? And I didn't realise – being golden – that my fascination lay in how far and how fast I would fall. Money? Sex? Friendship? Politics? Time went on, and those things lost their power to hurt everybody. Money and sex came and went, would come, might come, should not come – everything had its cycles and its moods.

'What made me fall, instead, was goodness. I was quite useless, quite isolated, hopelessly useless. Irrelevance.'

Jack intervenes: 'This isn't a story, it's the sin of pride.'

Anna goes on, 'And so I took up with Jack. I moved with the times, and fell behind them. I became a minimalist, suppose. And my mother felt she'd lost me, and with me she's lost something nearly perfect. And she shut herself away. To try to keep something of that perfection, that horrible, non-communicating perfection. And I could have gone and got her out. But I didn't. I thought, "Right: it's your turn to be the golden girl, not me" – and I have the key. I have the key to her house. And I don't use it.'

I think I was right about Anna as avenging angel, also a bit funny, a bit odd. 'I see your freedom is a terrible weapon,' I say, 'and ambiguous. But how does your key help us to get out? And what has this to do with people here, in this city?'

'The key means: deciding to be free, or to take the prison of others on yourself, involves a loss, and not only for yourself, for others. Perhaps most of all for others.'

'Yes, Anna, it's a nice, a fine, a very fine point,' says Jack. 'But remember, stories are not just to get us out – or make some exchange with who put, or keeps, us inside: this is a real prison, real walls and so on, where there seems no chance of communicating with anyone at all, except each other. So – either you communicate usefully with us, or with someone else – or you must expect your story to be judged, since judging is also what happens in the context of a jail.'

'Yes,' says Helen, 'Just who got us in? Since there's no charge, an agent is the clue. It's no doubt Alex, with his contacts.'

Jack knows how true this may be, but keeps quiet because he's jealous of my powers. Even if my powers have got me locked up.

My turn for the story. 'Perhaps you expect a story of high politics, like Jack's. Or family happiness – family tragedy, like Anna's: which after all I do like. Or Helen accepting her limits and with them setting bounds to everyone else. But mine is a very simple tale, that I heard here. There was a wedding, not so long ago. The cars with furry dice, the nodding dogs attached by their eyes which lit up, to the brakes. The flags, the processions, the dancing, the feasting on what will be, from now till eternity, slender pickings. Always less than what the culture once offered. The difference being, as regards everywhere else – where the culture too is running down, bellies are smaller, lambs are thinner, the drums and clarinos wheeze and thump – that the loss here is felt more keenly now. So, while Mr Modern laments that his star is hitched to a feudal donkey cart, the people on the donkey cart itself complain: "never such a load, or such an unwilling mule, never so much dust and such deep ruts ..."'

Jack is impatient. 'Trivia, Alex.'

'Running down, Jack. Everyone calculates in terms of solar energy. But what about human energy, Jack? So, anyway, this couple settle down, life becomes normal. again. And one day the husband comes home and says, "I'm sorry, but I've lost you." "?" she says, naturally. And he, "I've lost you to a cousin, playing bones."' (A game with knucklebones, I explained.)

'She is very upset, but realises he can't renege on the deal, as this would also be doubly degrading for her. And her new man says, being a decent sort, 'I really don't know what to do with you.' So he loses her again at cards. And at this point, it becomes a matter of honour, that she be passed down and around in this way. No one can make her his wife, because that would be an insult right back up the chain, and also degrading for the last person, since the poor girl at this point is just a walking poker chip.

'So, the question is, how to change the culture? Publicity is suggested – which would expose the practice, but not help the people involved; and anyway, the practice is diffused, and if only the first winner had taken her to bed instead of being decent, things would have passed over – unsatisfactorily, no doubt, but over.

'Normally, one would have quietly sold, or lost her back to the original owner. But it was just that transaction that was now impossible: the woman, and other men and women said no – the circle couldn't be broken, and reformed, in this way. Unfair on everyone – gamblers and wives alike. There was only one way out.'

Jack said, unnecessarily, 'Alex, none of this matters. Everyone knows it doesn't matter. We are not allowed to say this, but people matter if their plight attracts powerful people. What the powerless do between themselves, what they have done to them is now and always quite irrelevant. And will you never understand this? Not understanding this simple fact has screwed your own life up, and sent you chasing impossible dreams, impossible causes.'

I continued: 'The way out was this. All the men who had been part of this chain of chance combined to lose her back. Then, to avenge her honour, and their own, they killed the husband, just as he'd got her back.'

'That sounds like my story,' said Anna. 'Or like mine,' said Helen. 'And not at all like mine,' concluded Jack, 'but mine was more entertaining.'

'In that way,' I went on, 'the culture was not broken, the guilty husband was punished, honour was saved all round, and the woman was free to choose – or not – a more skillful, or less impulsive, gambler for a mate.'

*

We stayed locked up for six days. Jack, I think, could have roared his way out – but he was afraid of leaving me, and leaving Anna. Or perhaps his will had already been drained by being part of the trussed and waiting parcels in my spider's larder. We were bundled out one night, a wooden door, like a fence section, closed into anonymity; behind us we left another meal of peppers.

No one suggested further protest. To cause embarrassment, finger specific interests would – as I hoped my little tale had shown – have left us to pay for the first, and not the last, act in the chain.

Jack wanted to leave. He said, 'I don't care any more who's organising these demos and these plots. It's all a backyard question. Nothing to be had for any of us here – not you, Alex, and not me. Let them sort it out themselves.'

When we had left the prison, I noticed that the muezzin on whom Jack each evening tried to fix his position, had completed his circuit. Six minarets, at sixty degrees of distance each, had ringed the place we were lodged in. Those six days there had been a pattern, as though a full revolution had been made. I'd never found before a logic to 'his' movements – or 'their movements'.

I walked to the watchman's cafe. It was closed. The notice of closure had been taken down. Something about our jailer brought him into mind. He might have been a cousin, but the belly was the same. A holster buttoned down, a stick for tapping donkeys his only visible weapons. On a pole there was a poster, perhaps for the singers I had seen – the best. It had been printed, it said, at Kukës, over the border, but the printshop's name was torn – it looked like *bafra*, or it might be *bagra*. *Bafra* was a make of Turkish cigarette, and *bagra* was a gang in Serbian. I felt an obscure joke was being played: on whom? It could surely not be me.

I remember Helen's comment as we left the jail. 'An odious person, betraying your friends, your principles, their principles.' I think she was talking to Jack, but it may have been to me.

Outside, everything had recomposed itself, toughly, taking thought and heart. It always seems this way, daunting, when one has been released – even if jailed for, precisely, your principles, your friends, their principles. Betu was triumphant when I saw her. 'Such a long time!' she said. 'And for what?'

'You know for what,' I said. 'And did you manage to sort things out, get things started?'

'We can do anything here,' she said. Ingenuous, alarming, arrogant. To be expected in six days, a long time in anyone's life. As Jack had often told me, 'The trouble with you, Alex, is you believe all that crap – internationalism, atheism. Take it easy on yourself.' And so, to keep Jack out or to make things tough for Jack's friends and their money, I stand, awkward and a bit ashamed, on the side of integralism and feudalism. Meanwhile Betu is not sure whether I am more a hero or a crook: I think she'll decide for crook – it's easier. Something between us has been lost – there is a new intimacy, but too close to complicity – wife with a husband turnip-drunk in a ditch.

'Betu,' I say. 'The answer to your problems isn't in the music you choose.' She says,

'I don't look at problems, or solving problems, in that way. One must take a stand,' and I suppose she's right. After all, Jack's lot invent diseases and spread them around – can't take a stand against that, only against Jack. The real question isn't here though. It's seeing the buildings coming down in dust, and thinking – well, so we shan't need them again, or – well, they weren't so solid after all; even – thank God they've gone! What's impressive is not the problems you can't solve, it's the certainties gone. What's behind them? A beautiful view – a bit naive, that. A big hole? much more likely. A big hole with skeletons and catacombs and beetles and albino rattlers and broken sewage? Now we're getting there. When old Herzen wrote, it was always about the challenge – which perhaps we wouldn't meet – of building new structures – which might not be as classy, aristocratic, as the old. But he had never worked on a demolition job. There will never be that beautiful view. We may never fill in that dank hole. We may end up in it ourselves. We may be forced to live in it. We may build a replica of what is already built around us.

We may go and live there, Betu and I: Helen and I. Anna and I. Helen and her deadlines. Anna and her woodshed, where she spent her childhood, preparing for bonfires. Betu, much more successfully, more stupidly, preparing to live where the alternative to apocalypse is not hope and passion, but the everyday. Scraping peppers for the roasting.

Classifying: Anna, with money, but in the end no class. Helen – a nice girl, gone to newsprint, alas. Lots of honesty, even too much, always interesting these days. Sombre thoughts, because this whole scene is shortly going to blow. Not just the faceless manipulators here – the famous leaders behind the scenes who disturb the primal innocence of the masses on the march: but – well, you just can't treat your friends like that, Jack and Alex ...

When suddenly, there's a tape of good old Jorge Ben! Singing a song naming African gods as if he believed in every one, and now changes to one about – can it be, a marlin in Paraguay, sliding up into a high yelping, with somewhere a winged accordion and high warbling girls like blue fruit bats. Beautifully engineered that sound. Old friend, that sound, old fraud, Alex, names of gods and names of girls, all good for a song, and every shape of percussion, like a superchef twangling and beating every shape and surface in his superkitchen.

It's Red, with a tape. I ask, 'You like Jorge Ben?'

'Who?' Red is interesting because of his problems, but has only his problems to recommend him.

I feel kin with the walking wounded of the Enlightenment, waiting with them for a cleansing wave. I too have defended the indefensible, not protested at what was done in my name, the name of my countries, parties, principles; like you, my peers, my brothers. Where can we all repent? The deserts would be full of penitential columns, each with a squatting, half-self-redeemed saint, the caves full of sore-headed beatified bears, moving towards sanctity, leaving the public world, its smoke-filled rooms, behind.

I say swiftly to Red, 'I arranged with Betu to have us locked up so that Jack and the Americans would not meddle in your people's affairs. I shall do my best to stop the Soviet Union backing the Serbians or anyone else. This is the message – non-intervention – that I've fed Helen with. Anna is a talking doll. I am the traveller who comes to the castle, wins his case, serves a term as mayor of the village, and runs off with Betu, if I haven't scared her off.' There, it's done. Confession is lovely, and so is boasting.

Red says, 'I don't understand – I couldn't hear.'

Good boy, Red.

Betu comes along, high on herself. 'I shall sing for my own people, I shall inspire them, make them aware of my heritage, their heritage – a people like the Celts pushed for too long to the margin.'

'Yes,' I say, 'You're right. Nothing more to say. This is the right choice for you, the global audience, the other would bring you only regret and isolation. What is the use of an anonymous, inattentive public? What does it serve, to be discovered and discussed on tape, after your real death? You must give now, unstintingly. Yes, I'm convinced you're right.'

Perhaps she will make it to be 'THE BEST', perhaps for a moment the hands will lie hushed round the beermugs, the trip to the lavatory – into the lights and past the performers – postponed.

But while she was undecided, there was a space for me. And now? The uncles are all pleased. Everyone is pleased. Another choice was never really on. All her life she'll be able to tell her orchestra what she wants them to do – not like the Met. And hire and fire them, too. And I envy the watchman as well; able to discover, as all watchman can, a bar that's always opening just as the favourite one winds up: always hearing Betu.

'Betu,' I tell her. 'You must remember that this being marginal depends not on you, not on your society, but on balances and forces elsewhere.'

'That's why I must work here, work as hard as 1 can.'

Good. But I have left something boiling on the fire, and, I fear, I've eased myself out of Betu's intimacy. A habit of mine – or realism, a sane prudence?

'I should have liked to stay here, with you,' I tell her.

'That would have been very nice,' she says.

'No, really. It is a chance, another chance, I've missed.'

'But,' she says, 'the people you work for would not have liked that.'

'It all goes that much deeper, Betu. I should stay with you here. Make my life with you.'

She is a bit convinced. She says, 'It would not be so impossible. It requires conviction, courage, perhaps. But you have things to do, important things, and those you work for ...'

And if I tell her, no, I work for no one. I'm settling old scores, doing what I feel is required, by the logic of a position which does not actually declare itself, does not in vulgar terms actually *employ* me or *instruct* me. Does not, in terms that are ever more vulgar, or more neutral, necessarily *remember* me, nor, if it did, would *trust* me. Masters, that is, who want things on the cheap – at least from me – and so rely (if that's the word) on freely given, and provisional, loyalty.

And if I approached this far, what would she imagine – Moscow? Tirana? The Latter-Day Saints? It all becomes too ludicrous to mention, and more to the point, any answer, moving near or away from a hypothetical truth – is quite impossible.

I mutter something about my family ties, my Albanian forebears, the Macedonian grandfather who was useful further South.

And yet, to say I am in no one's service save my own reading of historical logic, of historical force, is quite impossible – reduces me in her eyes to a mere owl, nocturnal silhouette: the bird of wisdom hooting and honking like an idiot, and quite incomprehensible. The idiot with the family.

'When 1 was young, or younger, I knew an Indian girl,' I improvise, hoping that curiosity and some jealousy will bind these crumpled bricks together: 'And from her I established a distance, quite unwittingly, which reflected, I suppose, my feeling that her world would, if it knew me, reject me as being alien.' (I remember the panel truck: Jean Tremblay, the kids saying 'not a crazy Frenchman, but a crazy Indian'). 'I didn't want to make the same mistake with you.'

And she replies, as certainly she should, 'But we all like you.' She is at home here. And my Micmac knew she wasn't.

'What was she like?' she asks.

'Well, she didn't smell of cinnamon,' I begin, then I think, 'Jack must be quite mad, or else he's left his buddies, taking Anna round glistening like a big rich bun.'

But Betu thinks I'm being rude: 'It doesn't bother me – I know you've been in love a hundred times. It'd be odd if you hadn't.'

The minaret at our backs is suddenly alive with voice. No one is visible. Is that a disc of white there, a swaddled head? Or another of the agentless gestures – those pulpits in churches reared up like prows of ships, out of proportion, an arrogant sextant shooting up, convexly arching in the sanctuary. A headless voice, a preacherless pulpit. The Muslim pulpit in the Christian basilica.

'Betu, I should go and spend some time with my friends.'

'You have friends here. Why are you afraid to acknowledge them?'

I am embarrassed, 'Yes, they are more than friends, they are true comrades. They have risked a lot for me.'

'Well, we shall also hope that when they agreed to lock you up and look after you, and stop Jack doing what he might have done, the risk was repaid. You kept your bargain. And in any case, friendship remains, not counting profit and loss.'

'Yes,' as I speak, I notice the call of the muezzin is followed by a silence, as of no feet, no people wending their way to prayer: as if the hours were striking, a mental chit signed to mark their passing, a lost obligation, a further distance from a duty – outworn? Respected? I must admit, I didn't know, I didn't care to know, what link there might be between the ritual and its mysteries. certainly in Betu's songs there was little of the mystical: rather, good healthy peasant stuff, fixed firmly a century ago. The centre of the world was still the oxcart; with perhaps a train or telegram serving its mechanical, dramatic role.

'Your friends!' says Betu. 'You don't treat friends like that. To have them all locked up, and Jack kept quiet!'

One feels most regret about the plans that work – or, at least, most uncertainty. I had gambled and the horse had won – the winnings seemed more problematical.

'I feel we are all, though, still in danger,' I admit: 'Jack has been put off my track. Jailing us both has justified his judgement: that here, it's stalemate. Not worth getting involved. The liberal case will win. Things will work themselves through. The loans will come, or they will not come. Your neighbours will fear you or despise you, see you as enemies – we hope not much will change.'

But this is stardust, and she knows. My actions mean I'm not sceptical. Indeed, I feel I've done the biggest thing I knew – against my brother, and who was once my friend, Jack. And with the perfect, liberal witness, Helen. And Jack was here to do my job: and watching me, he failed to watch the real game going on, in courtyards, at the fields' margin. Isn't that enough – to stop Jack doing what he might, he could, have done? And all the rest is feet of angels trampling above, enormous shanks, tunics like kilts of light and lightning, so immense and complex you can't look up far enough to see what if any reason there was for all that fuss about their sex.

And this, by processes of doubt and elimination, should have left me to be free with Anna. But instead – that she is unencumbered unattached, now seems a vice and not a virtue. The good gangster always gets the innocent, in fiction; in fact, he would be lucky when all debts were paid, to make it with the ostler's widow, husband precisely plugged while carrying a bucket.

'Alex,' Betu says, 'you must get away. Your Macedonian grandfather would be a terrible responsibility for you now, if you are caught. To explain why you are here, and meddling – you understand, your position would be even worse than Jack's. And this time, there would be none to help. Not governments, nor shadow governments, neither those who believed you, nor those who didn't.'

In fact, I shudder at the thought of explaining. All sex and intrigue, nothing happening – and yet, my own fate, fate of historic peoples hanging, or dangling, on my words. Icecream. Beefsteak. Imagine the explanations.

'No, I must go back and see them, find out about their plans.'

A television is showing a huge demonstration somewhere but the picture breaks and slides. We see the flags, but it's not clear if they're green or red, or whether the little stars are white or black. The faces, too, could come from Africa or from Belgrade. I think I see Milo on the platform, pigments reversed – perhaps proposing a new great Trek, leading his oxcarts up the Rhine, stealing the Volkswagens from the locals, a massacre of Zulu chieftains in the Bundestag. The waiter in the restaurant pounds on the television, producing a mesh effect. He turns to face us, looking in the window, our faces pressed against the glass, clowns. Flips the channel, and there's an old clip of Jerry Lee Lewis with a head of steam, phasing from black to white and back again.

There is a note left at the desk. 'Dear Alex, we must leave in haste. We feel your presence is a dangerous one for us, but also for yourself. It should not have been Jack that they locked up, but you. And you will do better on your own – we shall head South, so you should try the North. Helen will wait some days and then she'll explode her piece. She calls it "Revivalism, patriarchy, and the economic year zero". I feel there's too much in it, but she says that is just the point. Jack says to say "Ta ta old scallywag, see you on the Reichenbach Falls another time" – he's really sad to see you go, we both will miss you so. It's too bad, Alex, that you have such commitment, and such fire. Jack is taking it all very laid back, he says, but you are like a steam-horse – I mean a battle-engine – ha ha. But we must hurry. Goodbye, dear Alex, you will always be my special person. I shall keep you where I keep all my special people, and never, never forget you. Next to staying with Jack, not staying with you is my greatest sacrifice. Love, Anna.'

Well, I had escaped her Bluebeard's Castle. *Alles leben* – but not much.

I run to Betu's house. 'Look, I must become a traveller again. And this time it really is a winter's night. Who knows what japes Jack has up his sleeve?'

The lights in the cakeshops and the wreathshop are hard at the centre, but blob out like honey: naphtha. A little line of popes twists to avoid a skein of imams.

Betu is enthralled. All the world loves a fugitive. But she says, 'After all, you've done nothing: even paid the hotel bill, which is the most important thing of all.'

'I know that,' I say. 'But don't say I've done nothing, I have composed my charge sheet, reckoned in terms of how long, not how much.' I think for a moment of the border, the splendidly and newly painted roofs of warehouses on the Albanian side, a blue of such uniformity and innocence.... But how can one even think of that?

'No, no, that's quite absurd,' says Betu: if on a winter's night a traveller, scrambling across the frontier, if that were possible through so many conditionals ...

'I shall come with you,' she asserts.

'Thank you,' I say.

'At least to see you safe away.'

'I thank you, but of course … and where should I, should we go?'

'Of course, I'll see you safe,' she says. Good words, indeed, the best.

'It's better I go North,' I say.

'You must get a ride, but it will be rather hard.'

I say, 'Perhaps I could just get picked up, roll on all night in someone's truck.'

'They're all locked up in parks at night,' she says.

And how far will you come? The further North 1 go, the safer I shall feel, but for her it's the opposite, ride into dependence and precariousness.

I start to say, 'But it's so insecure,' meaning for her, but she just sweeps me on, and says, 'I can have friends anywhere, as long as the driver's one of us.'

Grimly and silently I say, 'They're all locked up in parks at night.'

We run, all arms and legs, out to the road, sliding on the leaves, street lights there for the record, not illumination. She pulls me along – dogs are amused, then angry, then just interested. Throwing up my arms and falling in a hole, I make a fine woodcut with my silent word-balloon of 'help'. Somewhere a man is shouting – he might be a watchman. I think he is saying 'criminal', but she says 'name of his dog'. We panic along.

Then we were clear of houses, and alone. I saw the broken kerbstone was a pink, marble slab, like they had in old family grocer's, or as if a pig had once been bled there.

She is close to me, so close that I embrace her and find we were embraced already. So, life is off and running again, but we're too winded to follow on. We hug each other. And I said, 'We must get a ride on a truck. If not, we're finished, almost before we're started, cut off, without another ploy or plot.'

'I told you, at night they're all locked up in parks.'

'Well then, my dear,' I say, 'We must stow away, or steal one. Otherwise the story stops here, ignominiously – and I may never hear you, singing like a bird ...'

'I told you. At night. Locked up. In parks.'

'There is always some way, some way to get what you want when you're sure of it. No one can stop traffic all night. Think, Betu. Or at least we must get into the parking lot, cut through the fence. Just think, how we can do it.'

I am thinking fiercely, theft, hotwiring, plea of insanity, a good lawyer.

'Yes,' she says calmly, 'we must get into the lot.'

'But how? At night. Locked up.' She considers:

'Sometimes the watchman is drunk.'

Rome, 1990

Coney Island

> The high hills are a refuge for the wild goats, and the rocks for the coneys.
>
> Psalm 104: 18

I

'I KNOW the sun will rise again,' he said.

It's laying its wobbly belly down, flabby and liquid; up shoot the darts, the spears of gold, as he, the big one – down he goes to rest. The scene is pink, but then the watchers, the public, the stalls, all goes to dusk and now to dark. What to do? Sleep too? Go home? Drinks?

This guy's torn between some clowning, some magnificence – he conducts the last chord, air orchestra. 'Look,' he said, 'I'll leave the last note hanging on – the cellos ...' and his girl, eager, asked,

'What do those look like?'

There was no particular sound that hung around.

She said, 'It's so natural. But – those striations that must be furnace gas. It's green. Purplish too. But otherwise yes, it's a wonder, coming from somewhere, with no help. And your conducting it,' she added, anxious to please, 'Accomplished.'

Should he shrug her off? He made the calculation. No, there's advantage still.

Well, she thought, he is pompous. That would need work.

'When the snow had come to stay,' he said, 'maybe you remember, down by the river. The gypsies dancing? The cakes, the clay dolls? I mean – the Rom. No, they can't have been, of course, not real ones. Vagabonds – but dancing.'

'No, I don't remember,' she said. 'Surely you don't?'

'Something about lingering,' he said. 'Music. Surely you remember?'

'Honestly, no,' she said, 'but I could try. I picture. Yes, there's the scene, but you don't fit.'

'It was last year,' he said. 'We weren't together.'

'Well, that makes it nearer,' she said, unconvinced: 'They say something's been broken, maybe that's why remembering is hard. Before we were born.'

'It's always breaking,' he said, boldly, 'and being made good. It's evolution, only people don't see it.'

'No, this time, it's really cracked, they say. You

mend it one way – it breaks worse the other.'

*

This is a centre. Centre of shopping. Here, there's no eats, but big trucks keep dropping off big crates. The guys, the gals, they rip them open, take what's in. As if all had been discounted earlier. The two I'm following – they chirrup as they steal, and put stuff in the other's knapsack. They can't reach their own. Like special birds, they are, some special way of mating.

Other guys run from the stores, and beat the crowds with sticks, but mostly there is stealing here – the stuff is poor. It's underwear and boots, electric stuff to throw away – if you didn't like to steal it, wouldn't be worth a spit.

The lights – those are the thing. They light you up like gelatines – the red, the strawberry, greengage green, the blue of deep-down eels – they make the faces blob like jewels. The music – there's a sax, and then it's organ, choirs for a funeral, and doodyblueit swells to paradoodumwaah, and fades away – don't need to listen, just dusts over you with mood.

I've done my trades, you're 'buys' or 'sells'. Buys is the best, of course, and twenty minutes is your day. I've bought a property, parkland all round. Yunnan, I think – of course, I'll never go. The price includes the staff, they're paid for life.

'Hey,' said the girl, Pippa, as I found out, and points at me – 'That guy, some freak, he's following us ...' her guy's not interested, says it's always so. Pippa – she wore some shoes with flowers, a dress with different ones, a little bag for stealing jewels and such, all flowered with different styles.

I told them, 'I'm not just mansions. I'm lots of other things. Of course, I make mistakes as well – casinos for the Arabs ... that was bad.'

'But they're yours, the mansions?' Pippa asked.

'It's a fine point. Money went in. But, of course, you'd never live in them. Too complicated. And why should you?'

Pippa's into bondage, I soon learned. She seems a nice dull girl. It is all piloted – some guy that ties her up, according to the book, then gives her sex. Her guy here smiled at her, and scowled at the idea.

'There's this fine guy,' she said. 'Knows about it all, instructs, and doesn't let you die. It's for weekends. It's just like jumping off a bridge.'

More crates arrived. I said, 'They never tire, and yet the stuff's the same. Why're they so fired up?'

'Guns, I expect,' she said. 'That's what they're hoping for. It's what everybody does.'

She explained: 'With ropes, the sex is good. Not huff and puff.'

Her guy – she called him Stark – some name! – he

turned away. I guessed he's got some secrets too, to spread around. She reached her crucial puff, and he had got his huff ...

He told me, 'Being a couple – it's a thing you try, accepting danger, when you're very young, but in a while you learn to fix things up yourself.'

I said, 'Don't be afraid. I'm curious. So long as I'm a buyer, I have time. And there you are, attractive people – time to watch you both pursue your happiness. The goodness, respect for self, maybe for everyone – you'll juggle all that stuff ... Of course, if I go down from buys to sells, next step's the street, and then farewell.'

They're not convinced. Not by my whim, my idleness. My cash. What could it mean – this couple rooted in themselves, what could my riches mean to them?

Stark wore a singlet, like a flour sack cut down. It said 'Scorpions'.

'My brother's,' Stark said.

'You don't need to apologise,' said Pippa. She put her arms round me, gave a hug, then more, little ones. 'There, do you feel better?' she asked.

I didn't answer.

'We could adopt you,' she said, a silent asking towards Stark.

'No, no,' I said, 'I'm the driver here.'

Stark wound up his arm and turned, and practised throwing air – it could be rocks or footballs.

'Go easy with relationships,' I warned: 'Naturally, I'd be against some kind of system: – this stretch of life, is a soft dive – like, you go on till there's a turning, then you must decide. Onwards or upwards.'

'If you're just another psycho, trundling down the road – staring at us, our lives – you're waste. You're just an ogler,' Pippa said.

Then Stark, who'd pondered, reared up and said, 'There is a purpose. Of course. All those people, who fight and don't submit, untidy too – the thing is, the purpose always lies behind, it's in time past. There's purpose, but not now: you only find it when it's dribbled out, into uncertainty and impulse. Look back, and there it was.'

'You mean,' I said, surprised. 'The thing we cannot know, the past of others – that's the real, the only, object of our knowledge?'

'No, not of knowledge. Of certainty,' said Stark. 'But there it is, quite hypothetical. And real.'

'Well!' I said. 'That's where your scorpions come from, then! The tail raised, the sting accurate and misdirected at the beast's own head. The unknowable, the ungraspable – is always there, waiting to be known and grasped, and never is.'

'Those Scorpions,' said Stark. 'Just a bunch of

noisy guys.'

*

There – musicians, sitting in the roadway. Those ragas – seem to know a lot of what we can't quite say.

'Those squealy things,' said Pippa. 'Inside there's animals, or maybe spirits. Or,' and she wrinkled her nose, concentrating, 'the spirits of animals.'

Quite bright, I thought, but did not say. Stark said, 'It's only music. Not sticking to the time of day. Just on and on regardless.'

'Things may change,' I said. Suddenly, I thought.

'We could be moved on,' Pippa agreed.

'He means politics,' Stark said crossly: 'No hope there, but lots of hate. You move to the future when the now goes putrid. The smell lingers, it follows you.'

'I might agree,' I said, 'but it's best to say you expect transformations. Finding favours, doing the right thing.'

'Licking boots,' said Stark, 'till you see the blue moon in the toecaps.'

'We don't go far this way,' said Pippa.

'I can just watch you making some choice,' I said. 'It takes no time at all.'

'Of course, if it's just doing good ...' she said.

'I'm not so sure about that,' I said. 'I thought of standing a bit apart. Letting you choose. Though obviously I've an idea of who's the good and who's the bad. Even how that holds between you two. I keep that to myself, of course, until there comes the time.'

Stark said, 'You're ducking it. Us being good doesn't stop you pitching in.'

What a pain. I said, 'There's no doubt about the good and bad – not that can't be sorted out. It's the how, results, and partly there I'm at a loss, and partly…'

'When we've started, it's too late,' said Pippa.

'There's no place to start over from,' said Stark. 'You should be resigned.'

Pippa shyly undid another button on her top: 'Most people start by binding,' she said. 'It's the thing that most feels like being new.'

Her breasts were most attractive. But was this what I meant? And those things didn't last – the flesh, the spirit, both.

'Things lasting – that's quite different. Starting is one thing, carrying on is quite another – you take one mouthful at a time, or else you split,' Stark said. 'Eaten the food. Spent the money. Yup,' he said. 'Problems there.'

'That's why I thought to begin again, from the principles,' I said. 'Like choosing a couple, and studying them.'

'With that money that you make,' said Pippa, 'you

could feed lots. Starting with me.'

'It's not exactly mine,' I said. 'The funny thing – if I go and hand out food – I don't have any money! It just dries up. Like figs.'

'Not like figs,' said Stark patiently, 'those'd be just dried figs. It's the dry empty basket, that's what you mean.'

'He's not always this patient,' Pippa said, 'it's just he thinks you're harmless stupid.'

'Once you could sit a bunch of guys on horses or on camels and have them go off, telling tales, singing their song, and looking for adventure. Now, even climbing rocks – you need to be an expert – even how you fall. It's true, now we can all suffer in different ways,' I said, and Pippa interrupted.

'Not everyone. And suffering's a thing you're advised you should avoid.'

'Get the job. Do the stretching,' Stark said, and gave a dry laugh.

'There's too much "post-",' I said. 'Not mail. Just the present blocked, the past inaccessible,' and Pippa said, 'You wouldn't gladly go there, surely. The past.'

'No, absolutely,' I said.

'Out of the question, anyway,' said Stark, 'though you could try painting what you've got, fix it so. Decorate it. Engrave it. Act it out.'

'I've done all that,' I said, 'but it's not printing on

the paper that is hard – it's the breathing life.'

'You could do music,' Pippa said. 'The note book! – makes things resonate.'

'Nah,' said Stark. 'You have to let it flow. Remember the words, and clash out with your soul. What's the paper doing with all that?'

'That's all another planet,' I said. 'The paper. Industry. The law. Trying to collect your pay.'

'Perhaps you're right, and you should just watch us,' Pippa said. 'You know. At it. Me and Stark.'

'You're very kind. I don't think so. It's your little book of poems, after all. Best keep it to yourselves,' I said.

'It's bodies and gender,' Pippa said, quite stern, 'And being part.'

'I think I'd find it dull,' I said. 'Besides, you see it on TV. Crocs, rhinos – big stuff, and all well out of your way.'

'It's just – I want you to be free,' she said.

'And that's appreciated, you can bet,' I said.

And if the money's gone, and all the thought behind it? But Capital – does that disappear as well? And all the princes – turning back to frogs? No dawn, no roses blooming in the land – just those old buildings, books scabby-bound. Stark – his old shirt dustier ...

*

'Now, Stark,' I said, quite delicately. 'Don't misunderstand,' for he's a big guy, made of slabs and old clothes that would withstand another dirtying and rolling on the ground. 'But your grasp is weak. Language. You're not on to it. The language of reason and enquiry – you see it there. In the distance, blue and green, the terracotta towers. But there's no road that leads – you and your troop, your arms outstretched and all immobile. Why – the goats, the clouds – they move around, quite free – but ... You are stuck.'

He pondered this: 'And if I got there, and got taken in, the answers, free-living women, the chalices with red and yellow cherries, just like it was ... The table where they sat and ate their grapes, and maybe pressed a thigh. What then? You guys, ones that accumulate, and knowing nothing but the rolls of dice, you wear me down ... Suppose, instead of seeking purpose in the past, I just say it's been "fixed". What's past is frieze, and frozen on the wall. Describing it – it doesn't change a thing.'

'Naturally, Stark,' I said, humouring. He really had no idea at all. But my! he's big.

'We could find stuff in that house there,' said Pippa, pointing. 'Talking of mansions brings it out, the appetite. Collecting.'

'Oh no,' I said, 'you think of jewels, stuff to be carried off, new homes, but no! That owner guy's a collector, that's for sure, his stuff is worth a lot. But – it's just sounds. From everywhere, and some is old as old, and some from tribes that never wore a watch, the year goes round, then there's another, so it goes on for what we'd call some centuries, but for them it's one, one revolution, repeated till they die and then there's other guys, and other sounds that's just the same,' and so, I told them, it's just waves and noise, that's not worth anything but fills your days, and even has some history ... they didn't listen, didn't wait.

A crowd went by, and Stark and Pippa running too, 'another revolution', that's the cry.

*

I thought, 'I can't eliminate Stark – after all, it's just lust on my part, for Pippa. Besides, I feel they have to come to me, their choice, not have me interfere, though if they don't love me – Pippa – or admire me – Stark – I'd be angry. If they stop believing in me, I guess I'd be a kind of ghost.'

'You're only just a parasite,' said Stark, 'whatever you may be doing, or have done. You can't save us or protect us,' and I agreed. 'It's just my fun, observing. There's no point attacking me,' and at that Pippa looked quite sad.

'It's just the condition,' she said. 'You go with it or

hate it. Best to hope for cuddles,' and Stark snorted: You must make the first step, not just wriggle at the start.'

*

I was at my desk, fingers ready for the making of the millions. Soldiers must sit like this, and plan where their stuff will drop. It's worse for them – for them, it's playing battleships: you aim at barracks, hit a prison – it's not quite done to hate the other guys, or give them names or faces, or wives, or dogs or super racing bikes. Or clothes specific, shrines, or even languages.

I thought how what I did was clean, and just intelligent.

'Oh no!' Oh no – I hit a button, everything blew up – the one you never use, not buy or sell, it's Cancel. Me, the corporation, all those mansions, and I hear 'Oh no!', the guy that's next to me, that fringe of beard, he'd save his time if he just shaved, it's hair trimmed round his little mouth, like grass around a golf hole. You idiot!' he shouted. All his landscape's blanked.

'You've ruined us!' Up went the shout, some guys in suits, no ties, came running up. Their tools at once had lost their edge.

That was the truth.

I got called in – some guy, without charisma, never seen before. How had he got so high? Some tricks, acquaintances, no doubt. He said,

'Well, that was the lot, the whole, the yes and no, the good and bad. You cannot blame some flaw maybe there was, maybe you put it in. The beginning – that must have an end. Was there some moral gap that you fell down, maybe desire to see it all collapse around you, setting puzzles, more puzzles, neither you nor all the others round could solve?'

I'd like to blame the others, or the system – but, when all's done, I knew I was a party to the end, the finish, the last thing, with all the motivations cancelled, vanity and pride and anger, all the guys, their families, and stuff they had a plan to buy. All gone. The guy – his tag said Driver, maybe as a joke – sure, he's been wiped out too.

'To me,' he said, 'you're fecal matter. And I guess your parents too, the same material. And not just you and yours, but all your friends, maybe you had one of those, your lovers past and present if you'd got near to having some, psychiatrists hired to poke inside your fecal brain and muddle in your fecal dreams ...' and on he went.

'Listen,' I said. 'Just think – each end is a beginning. Our lives – they couldn't last, just sitting there and buying China,' and I stood and moved away.

Driver said, 'So! We're all adrift in your leaky boat – but it's you we'll eat first.'

*

Relations with Stark and Pippa – you might think them changed. Ruination. A black screen. I said to Pippa,

'Think – all those mansions, all over everywhere, unlived in and abandoned. Just go, take them, and live as we were meant. Tell your friends ... my blessing to you all, in need ... heedless and impersonal, the guys that bought this richness – forget them all. And me, forget me too. Live free upon the earth,' I said. 'And till the fields ...'

'Till, what's till?' asked Pippa.

'Till another lot arrive and throw you out,' said Stark, though he was impressed.

Some guys were leaving already – maybe they'd not needed telling. Only the lazy and the paired-off remained. So did Stark and Pippa.

'There went your bluebird,' I said, and Stark made a netting gesture –

'They flutter all around. Who wants to live in a squat in a palace,' he asked philosophically. 'Mowing lawns.'

'You're wrong to hang around here,' I said, but Pippa said, 'You must run into famous guys.'

I said, 'Oh no! An illusion, Pippa – the big fish, the talk that's always interesting, never memorable. That was all long ago. I thought – attack the markets, every day you come off best. And then you fall. It is the play, you understand. The lines are set – and yet, it's up to you. Forget or tumble, load the gun with ball not blank – it's life, dear Pippa, not just dragging on, but living it...'

Then I laughed, 'Come on, Pippa! – you can't believe that crap. Tilting at markets, armour, lances...! It's desk and buttons and guess. Methane, Pippa, that builds up, it has to find its outlet. Try sitting there, that's what grows and swells – and rocks the room.'

'That methane, it's a wonderful thing,' said Pippa. 'It makes auroras, storms on the sun. It even livens up the sunsets. It's red and green, and turns to hydrogen.'

Pippa knew all the science, details. That was good. Soldiers and religion – those are terrible things. I saw it on TV, they give no peace, and cost you bribes all year. Better know chemistry.

'We have neither religion nor soldiers,' said Pippa. 'And so it's better here. That's why we'll stay.' And she stared at me, and said, 'But don't try tempting me – I'm, in my way, incorruptible. And you – your error – can you be sure you didn't want to do it? Sink the ship?'

'Just an error,' I said, 'You're making them all the while.'

'It was more than that,' she said, 'a bad error. Down you all went, the good, the bad ... You should have watched yourself.'

'Myself?' I asked. 'My good self knew there was a flaw – that button, brought it all down, the fiddling and the ignorance. And Mr Driver too, that set it up and pushed it all along. My bad self – bored, and wanting all my mates should fall and scrabble round. What will they do, their kids, their debts? But – I know where the riches are,' I said, with satisfaction.

Stark interrupted, that he wanted the good life, worth more than riches … And it's true but here it wasn't relevant, and Pippa said my good self and my bad, they seemed parts of a whole that maybe wasn't up to it, and on she went: the nebulae, the neutrons frisking round, and all in swirl and ecstasy of palette, though these sodium lights sure cut it down, the mystery, the show.

'Perhaps,' I said, 'you should organise. Lessen your despair.'

'We are organised,' Stark said. Crowds moved around us, in rhythms almost circular. He said, 'They don't just do it in random,' and Pippa said,

'We keep rabbits too.'

There they were, in their own apartment block, the boxes stacked and private. Smelly but secure.

The russet ones, the velvet browns like handbags, all with that constrained hop that reminisced of fields and gardens – one hobbled hop to left and hop to right.

All too symbolical, I said, and, 'You're never going to eat them too? As well as prison? It's too much.' But Stark said, 'No, it's cruel before; and after, cruel as well; and in the present – respite. When we're hungry, it is us or them,' and Pippa said, 'If we're not in the mood, a guy will do it with an axe.'

*

Pippa rested a hand on my shoulder, and dipped a little, a kind of curtsey. 'Pippa,' I said, 'you're kind of interesting, your bondage, and your rabbits. Stark, though, seems to me a block, a rock in the middle of the road.' She considered, and said,

'You know how we value you. You, creator of the riches and the poverty, all-powerful and fallible. Stark calls you our Uncle Joe – but just in fun. It's you watching us, as if you'd never seen a human, beetling about, rolling the dung and storing it somewhere safe...'

'Is that what they do?' I asked. 'Beetles? It is new to me. Who would have conceived a thing like that?'

'Stark has his secret,' Pippa said. 'He's walked the world. He's fought and run, and sat by streams, and watched the bodies floating past, and then the boughs of red flowers and the white, the fish rear up, open their mouths as if to say the word – and sink, forever silent, to swim and frisk their tails ...'

'Yes, yes, I know all that,' I said. 'The faces at the wire, the tents, the huts – it's all gone deep inside each one, we don't know what to do – those images ... It makes you want to dance and stamp, a tarantella, yes, we have been stung, poisoned, bites all over, and out the poison comes, we dance, we dance, we try to shake it off, we scream, we roar, we twitch … But is this wisdom, Pippa dear? Or just the itch between our legs?'

'This is all cheap stuff,' said Stark. 'And the riches. Where'd they go, when you made your error?'

'Oh', I said. 'It looks as if they've gone, but they will pop up somewhere else. It's just – you don't have them any more. That's why Mr Driver's angry.'

Stark said, 'You're just a guy that pushes things along, like on a loaded cart. Fleeing something. Wonderful stuff on board – except you can't unload. Can't stop. You have to keep it going on, the chairs stacked up, the boxes locked. 'On, on,' you cry, 'it's not the journey, but the end that counts,' and there we are, all heaving, kicking our comrades out the way, our shoulders torn, and spit and scratch at who's beside – and there you are, behind, your shout is loud, your push is weak ...'

'That's cheap stuff too, Stark,' I said, 'And anyway, no cart, no push, no chairs potential. I screwed up, I admit – but it's the error you must punish, not me – I get you nowhere,' and he said,

'That's true, but there would be the satisfaction.'

*

'You? You, the big capitalist, knocked down capitalism?' said Stark. I thought – some sarcasm there. 'Well! Well done!' he said. 'And you say we should organise? When it's all done with a button?'

I thought the matter through: 'I wanted the best for everyone, win or lose,' I said. 'But at the moment, street wisdom – that is what I need. There's Mr Driver, wants some millions out of me, then there's living to be done, who knows how many years to go ...'

Pippa seemed sympathetic, maybe impatient too.

'I need to know, staying around this crowd,' I said, 'How you manage for order.' The rabbits turned towards us: I said, 'Think of all the humour went into those ears,' and a plump doe raised hers in a V.

'Of course,' said Pippa, much amused, 'Ears. We don't eat those.'

*

'I've no money, but I'm not poor,' said Pippa, 'So I needn't strip to live.'

Stark nodded: 'Now, men sing, it's women who

invent new work.'

Pippa said, 'Men and women? We're back to that, then? Stereotypes. Where's your eyes, Stark? Black and white, believers and empties – all that again, as over and over?'

Stark said, 'My eyes are good as yours. It's all about him now,' and he pointed at me, 'His Mister Driver. Everyone has one like him. We're the best here at keeping them away,' and I was pleased, though then he said, 'And now, it's time for us to hear – your philosophy. Your truth and justice, meaning of existence, morality – give us your take on that. You must have had the leisure,' and I said,

'Being a trader doesn't lead to truth,' and Pippa said,

'But here's a friend who has her own,' and there she was, Diane she's called.

Stark said, 'She's got religion,' and to her, 'Give him some of yours,' and Diane said, 'No, not religion, it's the faith, that binds and spurs, that gives a sense to everything. It's not the truth – who cares? – it's singing on, and chanting too, and that's the meaning, and it makes us all a band, a quest, that look for common things, and having them in common too.'

Stark exhibited her, turned her round and round before us, made her waltz a step or two. I asked, 'Can she make that Driver kneel?' and on she went, 'Not kneel but find horizon, yours and march towards', and Stark got bored and walked away, but Pippa stroked Diane, and there she stood, just like a sugar-stick. Quite convincing too, if that was what you want, to make societies and till the fields, together drink the wine.

'There!' said Pippa. 'There's some emotion – doesn't cost, not like the bondage, though I pay in kind! I am quite enthused – there is the meaning, there it goes, if that is what you want.'

Diane had walked off: she'd said, 'You mustn't turn around. You don't look round to see if others follow you, that is not the point,' and left us both alone, Pippa and I, and Pippa said, 'It's not for us, a faith – I don't know why. I quite agree with her – but then – it's that agreeing turns me off.' and Stark was far away, I kissed her hair.

It smelt of boiling rabbit bones.

They boiled the bones to make the glue. Stark painted icons, secular his content, holy was the form. He must have sold a few. 'You put that gunk upon the wood,' he said, and then, quite loud, and to the world,

'We're pigs in a pen,' he said: 'They let us out when they need us. Or let us in.'

'It's the condition,' Pippa said, 'We don't accept it. The condition here, and in the general. Here, I'm free – it's the only place to be myself. It isn't much. It's everything.' And she paused: 'Maybe living here to seethe is best, and what I want, I can. The worse would be, to have some guys to stand me in a line and give me soup and leave me there.'

Stark laughed and asked her where she got the soup: 'Oh, soup there is for sure,' said Pippa. She seemed convinced, she must have read the book, right to the end.

'Diane says "forget the truth",' Stark said. 'And you still have justice, meaning, and some living right. That's not bad – enthusiasm too.' A long pause, and before our mind there passed long files of monks, in colours various, some blowing horns, others bearing whips. He went on,

'The problem is – we don't believe. No, not a scrap. Our disbelief – that must be worth? Leaders? Guys we know, chosen by us to give us orders? Incredible! And others who come in with cops? Forget! And if it's that, or else – dancing round poles and ashes on our heads? You were a trader,' and he turned to me, 'And would you give a price for that, for any of it?'

'Stark,' I said. 'I must admit – it's all above me, that philosophy. It's spiders hunting up a tree, you see the webs, the filigree. But Stark – they dine on flies, and stuff quite finicky.'

*

'You've lost your powers,' Diane told me. 'Maybe you were too specialised, though you were titanic too,' and she smiled to make it seem less sour.

'We must find a place to live,' I said. 'That's practical. Stark thinks that all is settled – the meanings, Pippa isn't sure. You're quite appeased. Where d'you live? A house?'

'No, no,' she said. 'The houses here are built from catalogs. They're not real ones, you get dispossessed. It only means "I want" – and what? Peace?'

Stark and Pippa overheard, and shouted, 'Peace – no. Never! Till we're dead,' and Pippa said, 'Stark was captain of a ship, and then what's all you want is wind.'

We didn't pause at that, the captaincy, and was it slavery or drugs, or riverboating with banjos, we didn't ask, and Diane said,

'It's in the ghettoes that they build to last, and make the walls so thick you hide inside,' and that was true – and here's a wall, all painted up its height, all over like a book, an icon, it kept them out and in, it kept us out, but we peer in and there were guys round braziers, all singing songs and chopping sticks.

'That looks all right to me,' I said, and they, all three, they shouted,

'Happy? Behind a wall? No, not us, that's what the Yankees want – the happiness, pursue it like a beast and plant their knife – its head all dangling down, the tongue unhooked … No, no, we don't want death, we want the quest, and not the death of other beasts – one day we'll just lie down, our breath will stir the grass and send a wave that travels into nowhere, on and on...' and Diane said to me,

'You haven't understood,' and that was true, but I was tired of standing round, a failure, and having sugar kisses blown, unending waves, and all that stuff. I said,

'I'll bunk down on this straw a while,' but Pippa said,

'No, no, the straw will give you hell – you need the hay, it's soft as rabbit's ears,' and laughed.

*

'We're the lucky ones,' said Pippa. 'We know about germs, so here we're clean, and nothing smells, except the rabbits.'

'That's also how it was before,' Diane agreed. 'We'd nothing then, but now we know it's going to last. Like that, it's a relief to know.' Stark laughed,

'Well, at least it won't get worse,' and then I thought, oh no, what a belief! How he has fallen – I should know, my difficulty began just yesterday, already it is worse; and Diane said,

'The thing is – knowing who to bond with. When

we were rich, a god provided everything, but now it's tough. What you must do – establish a personality that's clear and isn't shared by anyone – and then we ought to find some people who've got more, and recognise us and our rights – so, it will start again.' She seemed uncertain. Stark said to me,

'You'd maybe like to buy this icon,' and he showed me, there! – little, suffused with glue, figure a vague red, and – 'There's a spirit too, that flutters round its head,' he said, 'I'm only at the start of my career, it struggles to come clear – but do not fear, that isn't God, it could be any one of us, or nobody at all.'

He didn't press the point: I told him, '"Work" is the unfree, inhuman and unsocial activity, creating private property,' 'abolish private property, and you've abolished "work"…'

I wasn't sure if he just worked, or 'worked' caged up in those quotation marks, or if we didn't work at all, and Stark said, 'What the fuck, the end is always private property – I don't have much, though, you can bet,' and so discussion ended. Pippa stroked him, – 'You put on too much glue, my love, you can't see the picture through, you put it on the wood and on the top, it's like a sandwich,' and Stark said to me, quite roughly, 'Quit thinking about work – when they want you, you'll just do it.'

All day, all night, there was music – music from

sticks and bones, and cans and cow horns, a feisty strum that need not stop, ever, till our time is ended.

Diane brought in a friend, Corinne. Diane boasted about us, 'There's Stark, a guy that's done it all, commanded, maybe could start things off again, right from the top,' and she pointed to me, 'Master of everything, until he fell. Pressed that button, flipped from positive to negative. Maybe there's powers there still, though not to bring it down again – but look, his evil sideways yellow eye, paws pocketed, the glance still fixed on Chinese palaces ...' and they both laughed.

Stark asked Corinne, 'Do you have hopes, like Diane here?' and Corinne hummed a bit of song, and said that drifting was the best, it wasn't true you go nowhere, the hell you do! you move, and do not sweat...

Corinne wears clothes with little windows in, that let you see some flesh, inconsequential, that's for sure, but if you're inclined to spy and pry – they're like blind eyes, you fix on them, amber and green, inward they look, indifferent to you, but draw you in. She asked,

'Pippa? What's her speciality?' And Diane said,

'She's like those solitary white lights they leave in courtyards, lighting up the scene, attached maybe to cops, a commissariat. Cut across her, she will smile, and then up comes running Stark or other guys, with laths.'

Diane told us, 'Corinne lost her hope, I fear. She was a while ago the Governor of Europe. Denmark, anyway. Good job done there – not an easy people, though you might think quite insignificant: know all about you and have rigid rules. She felt the challenge wasn't warm, and so she left and walked the world.' Stark interrupted, said he hadn't seen her, maybe they had missed each other in some fog.

'Of course,' Diane went on, 'she went from chancellery to bank and back. Not with the low types you frequent, young Stark,' and Pippa said it was one easy thing to run a place that's full of snow, a harder one to guide a caravan of yaks – and we agreed that it was true ...

I drew apart, and said to Stark, 'I like you, Stark, you seem a regular guy, no secrets and know everything – but you are just as tricky and as doubling up as Pippa. That's attractive. Diane, though, she just knows the way to spot the gods and choose between them, the potent ones, the less – and Corinne, well, she's done the easy thing, the being Governor of Denmark – coupla words here and there suffice, in Danish or it might be Swiss,' and Stark cut in,

'Corinne! I never saw her on the Tien Shan, and that's a place where everyone meets up, there is no other way, you walk the world, around you go, there's no alternative,' and he must know.

You press that button by mistake, the system drops, but soon there drift these precious guys around, you stand like pointer dogs, just a command, a flutter in the gorse – and off you'll go!

We looked in a hut where Kazakhs were watching TV: 'Kazakh TV is crap,' said Stark, and Pippa said, 'The music's not, but of course you can't hear it. They love their sleep,' she went on, 'They've a tape of the steppe they play all night.'

'Stark!' I said. 'What's that shuffle that you do?'

'I get it from the caribou,' he said. 'It's to save your energy.'

'Stark, you know everything,' I said, although the gait's a farce: 'Howd'you pick it all up?'

'To know everything, it takes about a week,' he said, heavily. 'Then you rest.'

'I know,' I said. 'It was my eighth day that I screwed up.'

'Boys' talk,' said Pippa happily.

'Those Kazakhs run the labour market,' Stark said. 'But it is us who keep our values. Our philosophy.'

'That's good,' I said. 'But Mr Driver's after me, he wants his millions. Never real, they were, and so I'll have to sweat for centuries. How they all believed in me! – and now, who knows what tricks I'll have to do to cast the spell again?'

*

This is the beginning, I thought; now, the way out. I asked Stark, 'You must have contacts, comrades on the inside? the outside?'

'All dead, man, and gone, and lost, silent, wherever they were and if they were ... We're left with these mad sheep—' and he jerked an elbow to where Diane and Corinne were discussing ends and meanings.

'They say we should follow our heart,' I said.

Pippa tested imaginary bonds and said, 'Don't look at me. I've booked the bondage guy, for everything.'

The music's ended. Now, we never sleep, it is too quiet – and here's the Sun! Stark stood atop a dusty mound and crowed: 'I can't tolerate this monochrome!' he said: 'Here he comes again, just like I told. All burnished, spluttering gas, just like he took a shower in flame! Hail, lovely creature! Our one true friend, always bustling through the day, breasting the clouds, even through the snow – a wink, a blink. A day's work done and off to drowse behind those hills – and leave the watch, the night, to us.'

It's true, the Sun he has his work, and tiring too. And not a buck to show for it – well, that rings truer still. We turned our faces to him as he rose. Stark raised his arms in greeting, maybe submission too, we heard him mutter, 'Another day, without another dollar too,' and I thought – we are His caribou, a-shuffling through a tundra, bright as white ...

The Kazakhs left their hut, and gunned their trailbikes – off to where it was they went.

*

Stark and I – we consider our alternatives.

We could be a group. Not singing, no one plays an instrument, nor sings. We can explode over the world. Mr Driver is our manager.

'There's lots of groups like that, like us,' says Diane.

'Diane, you're a terrible tart,' says Corinne, and giggles.

Stark says, 'No, no, this won't work, it's only interesting to music critics – and there's no music. You need human interest and drama. That's what sells you. Hands and arms in the air, all sweating.'

'No, it's style and expectation,' I say. 'Numen.'

Here's the bus, here's the bridge, up there's the northland. Another gig in the snow: this bridge must be the Skyliner. 'It's luck,' says Pippa. 'There is bondage all over, even in this opium joint,' and she beams her red eyes at us.

Diane says, 'She's hallucinating. Pippa, do you hear me?' and Pippa says,

'I see the human interest – Diane has a thing for Corinne, that's why all day she washes all their clothes.'

We ignore that. Stark says, 'The guys here, they're all soldiers, that's what you must do when there's no work, but you can't even kill someone, or else it all falls down again.'

Diane says, wriggling, 'No, Corinne, I don't want that, whatever ... You're just a whore, d'you know?'

She knows, for sure. That's enthusiasm, faith, in step, justly promiscuous.

The concert: celesta and shouting. Makes a middle page. We split up, we're still friends, though, still looking. That makes a middle page.

Mr Driver takes our money.

'What you guys need,' says Mr Driver, 'is a trip in a rocket. Explode you all over the world. I'll light the touchpaper for you – you can't reach it from within the shell.'

'I feel most terribly ill,' Diane says. 'But, oh, how I love you, Corinne.'

'And I feel something vague for you,' Corinne agrees. 'Though I've my career in politics, you know.'

'They're not following their heart,' laughs Stark, 'What they want's to party!' and the two light up, and cry, 'My Party!' though they don't both mean the same.

'In Denmark,' Corinne says, 'we swung like clappers in eight bells,' and then I think that maybe watching people doesn't tell you where they're making for – it's party time, and in we go, it could lead all towards destruction, and there is Mr D, he's the eternal cleaner, picking up the pieces, pieces of eight, maybe, and Pippa shouts,

'Yes, we'll be Corinne's court!' – the palace that we're in fills up with Danes in masks and nothing on at all, there's big ice animals that when they melt you dive into the water and grow strong. There's lots of flesh that's pressing in, some bulging down and blue and russet, some guys wearing only jewels and bangles, and I hear Stark cry,

'Well, here there are potentials, but no information,' and there's Pippa, treated rough, in tears, and Stark shouts, 'And you're sullying my Pippa too!'

I say to him, 'You didn't hit her, Stark, I hope, for it is party time, all should agree and hit no one. Opinions? – you will tell them from the vote we may take after: this is Corinne's hour, it's restoration time,' and all are taking pills and shooting bullets in the air and at the walls, some guys as tall as pines with brassieres lit up and blinking red and amber – they do a dance, and there's a cry – 'The group, the group' – it should be us, but we're sedated with the noise, and Stark whirls round and bellows like a moose, and all applaud.

'It's only politics,' laughs Corinne, 'but it pries deep into your soul and never ends ...' and that is true, the guys go on and on, they steam with hot and cold and shout, and Corinne cries, 'The party, let's hear it for the party,' and everyone goes wild and if they've money hidden on them – up in the air it goes, and gals are screwing on the floor like squirrels, and the guys are doing likewise, it's relax all round, and then Stark says to me,

'No, no, this is Corinne's fief, it's not for us, it isn't going to mend my broken parts.'

Perhaps he weeps. And what he says is true.

Stark says – that anyone who wears those pants of alligator skin that nestle round your crotch, of course they stand a chance in politics, Corinne was a governor among the best there's ever been, Napoleon and Hitler, they don't even show. I say we shouldn't judge the Danes, and Stark says no one's judging, not now or anytime, it does no good, it's like the warning scarecrows give, you stand and wait and nature flaps your arms, and if they've brains the ravens and the owls come down; he paints the history like painting walls, and then I say,

'Look, Stark – we should protest. This finance

capital has ruined me. To get my fortunes back, and maybe help you out, and in a secondary way those rabbits in their hi-rise too, we need to organise and make the system work in quite another way. You don't need genius, just some million guys with staves and maybe hardhats too,' and Stark says,

'Yeah, of course,' and laughs, and I insist,

'It's work and wealth – the best books say we make our pile, then give it all away or share it round at least,' and then Stark says,

'This work and wealth – I'm not so sure those two are linked. In any case, I'm not so sure I want the one or even both,' and then he says that here they've tried to make a Plan, and set up laws, and then in various ways the digging, all together, or digging half the day and then the painting class and drinking when the light has gone ... I say, 'There's something in the setting up, or in the working out, or in the guys themselves, or wanting guys or gals for sex, or flags or ancestors or golden plates that you dig up and tell you what to do, be happy and obey. It doesn't seem to work.'

'Stop!' says Stark. 'You're just an idler, all you want is getting Mr Driver off your track, and make another fortune for yourself,' and Pippa says,

'Hypocrisy is god, that's true. The things are set up in a certain way, and when they all fall down, with murders, floods and illnesses – you think of other things to do, like sacrifices, blowing horns, or marching off and stealing cows and sheep …'

I tell her, 'That's what they all say, it's so banal!' and she puts out her shiny tongue and says, 'Look at those two, Diane, Corinne – what they're doing, that's banal, but still they do it, and they chirrup too ...'

I tell Stark, 'Some things are both hard and easy that you need to do – like setting up a group, a party. And governing, like Corinne does, when people tell you what is to be done, avoid the massacres most times, that's easy and quite hard as well, I guess. Creating, like I did, those huge accumulations, of things bought, imagined, borrowed, all with infinities of futures curled inside – wow, that was hard. Although, the hours were good. And Diane too – the faith in what you don't believe, yes, it must be quite hard to keep that up. But Stark, you and Pippa, when we think of what you can contribute to us all, and do no harm ...'

'Yes,' says Stark. 'The doing and the giving – things you must accomplish but be very ponderous and prudent, since it doesn't come quite natural, or not to us ...They say that's what it's for ... Working for almost free, and being good.'

We lay our lives before us, they're like aprons made of chains, that hide our hairy passions – only the best will do, in public anyway – and suddenly Stark says,

'Here we are, on the massif, and all around are caves, and there's a future for us all.' I take him up on this, and say,

'No, Stark, it's mushrooms grow in caves, not you. Nor Pippa,' but he says he'll practise drawing on the walls, crude stuff but maybe no one sees, and Pippa says, well, how would she get her sex? – that guy, he wouldn't make a cave-call just for her, and Stark explains, you get a sled and off you slide, down to the town below, and Pippa says the rabbits would be overawed, a cave like that lies in their nightmare, and I ask her if she prays when they get slaughtered, and she says she thinks she is a rabbit, rather, though carnivorous. I say that it's a lousy thought, the cave.

First, we go to see where I screwed up: the Office, there's guys in there, quite frantic, chasing the cash that flew forever into space, they work all day and night, they eat cold french fries, and I say,

'This was my life, dear friends, till I screwed up, and started watching you and found ... my freedom and your charity.'

Then Mr Driver sees us, says he'll call the cops; and caves and drawing on the walls becomes a promising idea again. I say,

'Stark, what'd we do all day? Those caves is damp and dark.' He says we'd do what we do now, we'd track the stars and watch TV and sing the song of how we got there, that's the stuff you have to do, and Pippa says it solves the doing and the giving part, we couldn't do much anyway – if you don't do you cannot give, and so another vicious circle's found and broken like a spell.

So, here we are, we three, sitting before our cave. I see the frieze of rabbits running round the walls and off into the dark. The bones of the last living ones are bubbling in the pot. Stark says, 'We aren't nobodies.' He points to me: 'You made things disappear and die, and then you lectured on excess: and me – my icons could be everywhere. A better shake of the bag, that's what you need for reputation. Pippa's lifestyle – sex just a slide away, down there, but family life with me,' and Pippa cuddles up to him and says,

'Yes, and quite aggressive too.'

It could be after all that we are somebodies. An interviewer with a notepad's scrambling up the rock to see us. Here's Diane too, Corinne is roped and hoisted after – here we're clustered, the pot with rabbit bones sings on, the smell ... Stark says,

'The place may smell of rabbits, though there's none alive. And if it wasn't them, the place would only smell of us,' and that is true, and Corinne says she's waiting to be called, more governance, for everyone has said they want some gutsy girls, good legs, to lead them, not to interfere too much, and Diane hugs her – they're a fashion statement standing there and Diane says that even waiting is a chrism, angels accumulate and when you're called they will burst out, like woodworm from a desk, and bear you up, and guys will write your words on birchbark, or on porphyry ... on she talks.

The interviewer writes it down, and asks me, 'You! What do you do?'

'I'm working on a plan to save the world – but mark me well, I rule out human sacrifice, it isn't in our culture now. Of course – you have to wish you will be saved.' I put my face up close to hers and puff a little, till she pulls away. I ask,

'Do you wish to be saved, my dear?' and she is nervous, asks,

'Saved? What from?'

I say, 'From living in a cave. From being poor and being rich.' She nods and writes it down.

Stark says to her, 'Maybe we've said enough to be on the TV and watch us saying it? At least the "do and give" routine has passed us by,' and then the interviewer says,

'No way! You're so banal, for everyone now thinks to live in caves and draw on walls, or underneath the sea. Just look around, there's guys with goats in caves, they sculpt, at weekends lots slide down to town for sex and other liberating stuff. The system – it fell down, it's true, but no one thought of different ones, or propping up the old – besides, some foreign guys, while we were thinking what to do – they got a start that now they're far ahead and can't be caught.'

'I feel,' says Stark, 'this cave experience may be drawing to a close. I'm hungry still. We didn't think to bring the booze.'

*

We leave the cave, the rabbit frieze. 'How shall we live?' asks Pippa.

Stark says, 'We'll take the rioters' cast-off stuff. Wear, and then sell on. That serves for life, for if you riot and you steal, then you must go on, for if you stop, you're something else, quite different. As for eats – there's that dog salame, 97% is good, it says, only three is stuff for dogs, you spit that out.'

Pippa looks sad at this: 'We're on the dogfood now,' she gripes. Corinne is irritable, to Diane she says, 'You look like a horse in flight,' and Diane says, 'A horse's bottom, do you mean, my dear?' and Corinne says, 'It's just your hair, my love,' and Diane says that politicians cover up their breasts and legs, some such would be the best in current circumstance, those alligator pants are too outré. So on they go.

Corinne says, 'You know, the Danes, they have to ask me back – just as a social thing: I showed them how to party and – they have a secret I am sworn to hide!'

Diane says, 'Do tell,' and Corinne says that when the Danes all went and lived in Iceland, there were people there, not myths and giants at all. Those natives stayed from when the world was warm – the country's central-heated now, but with the cold the Danes had made them stoke the boilers underground. 'Of course,' says Corinne, 'they are held in slavery,' and Pippa says, 'Who told you that, Corinne?' and Corinne says,

'Italians in a bar. It must be true, they had no interest to lie.'

Pippa sobs, the tale is bleak, and then she says to Stark, 'We should have done cave-dwelling right,' and he replies, 'There'll be another time,' and that is true.

I say, 'We look for depth in guys and gals like you: it seems there is not much. Maybe it seethes beneath the crust, like Iceland's slaves,' and then I say to Pippa, 'You are normal to a fault. Is there some love for me – we need it so, they say, and me especially,' and Pippa laughs and says they're used to having me around, but now's the time for swords and shields, and finding enemies to castigate. Till now we're only having wars against good people and the evil bands – now we should face real armies, foreign states. And all agree, we're on the trail of evil now, we've languished in our own excess too long, and Stark brings out a bottle, says that we should toast.

'Now we know what Kazakhs do,' he says, 'They make this stuff,' the label says it's 97 proof, and Corinne says, 'I love those Kazakhs. When their homeland has a vacancy, I'll answer to their call.' She swigs some vodka down, and then some more, and we all drink and think of battles, heroism, and evil overcome.

I try to rouse them. 'You're all so different, uncoordinated, so sadly normal in your ways.'

Diane protests: 'We try. You – you don't engage. You saw it all, how it was, when you were young. It couldn't be improved, you thought, your way.'

'No,' says Corinne. 'The trouble is, he doesn't pay.'

'For what?' I ask. 'Pay?'

Stark says dismissively. 'He wanted praise for winning. Then, praise for losing.'

'Well,' I say, 'maybe I'd help you train for Armageddons – not one battle, a campaign, I promise you.'

'All those prejudices,' says Pippa. 'And no history. Ancestors – you need those – they're a chain. That's what I find in bondage – a continuity. Did you even have a parent?' she asks me.

'I don't think so,' I say. 'If I did, he was just like all the others, just like me. And, Pippa, let's be frank. You look for sex, not genealogies,' and then they shout, and list regimes I didn't struggle with, the usual talk of massacres that slid past underneath my nose. I say, 'A person can't just intervene, in everything, and rise each day and say "how terrible" – yesterday, tomorrow too. It's vapid, don't you see?'

They're not appeased – and nor am I.

11

STARK says, 'It was no big deal, starting all this off. But the things that weren't foreseen! Those sheds,' he points, 'For big animals. Then something molten crashing through the roof ... Must start again with tiny ones. Breakages! Slippery fingers, try again, and at last it's us, created with big heads, unsteady on our feet, back-tweaking design, those flappy arms, the legs stuck on as afters – and now,' he rounds on me, 'you say the way is fight, between us and the other guys, loot some women we can't satisfy?'

I say, 'It's true, maybe I'm too vindictive, and of course I've you, my favourites, who disappoint, but who I love: yes, that's unfair on all the rest. It's Mr Driver that's the cause. I haven't got the money that I owe, nor yet the happiness it brings, – yet he pursues.'

'There's other things than cash,' says Diane primly, 'like truth and knowledge, though you can exaggerate with those,' and Corinne says that if you haven't got the power, then knowledge means 'kick in the pants', and Diane sighs: 'Those pants ...!'

What is to be done? We ask ourselves. Philosophy we've tried, and getting rich, and trying something else...

'Rabbit sausages!' Stark says at last, exploding with the thought. I say,

'Is that the best? Why take it out on nature? Rabbits? True, we could make some cash – but think, if we were lions, sleeping away the heat, there on the savannah, waiting for our mates to bring our lunch,' and I see Stark, his eyes half closed, waiting for Diane to bring a steaming eland home. 'The cubs—'

'No cubs,' says Stark, decided. 'See, our problem is – it is our human nature not to have one – nature: not in ourselves, nor round about. We like to see it all shaved clean; we can live anywhere, in geodesic domes, on suns, or underneath the sea. That is our curse, we were created thus, trying to outlive disasters we have made,' and on he goes, there's no one near to blame for what is fixed and firm, and I repeat, 'If only we were lions, young Stark, you'd be our hero, maybe, with that mane, so coppery and locked with gel – could be a helmet ...' and he interrupts,

'You idiot, of course it is – a helmet. Guys come around, they're beating up on us. Long time ago, when toppling towers was in the deck of cards, I'd need my helm when we were under Ilium's walls. I, hero, warrior – but now, the very reference eludes ...' and I say,

'Stark, I must admit, I don't get what you mean, but sure, some body armour's what we need. Or some fine governance, though I don't trust Corinne,' and Pippa says,

'Come on, it's rabbit stew again for lunch.' As she has said through history, it's all been written down and sculpted into travertine. And so we eat – there isn't much.

*

'You two grouches,' Pippa laughs, 'you and Stark, wanting your unique thing. I don't worry – you can't be more unique than me.'

It's true – those flowers she wears – they've all gone jungly. Foxgloves – those pinched mean mouths, like wallflowers, their teeth – her bondsman should watch out, she's armed all over, the pollen deadly, anthrax, the pistils poisoned spears. 'Just flowers!' she laughs, 'And "bondsman" isn't right.'

Corinne says, 'Well, unique's my other name, and every day I'm getting more unique,' and Stark jumps in, 'No, no, Corinne, we've ruled out politics and states, and huddling in crowds and throwing cobblestones. The cops – they have electric vans, you can't burn those, their tasers brand you all your life, you can't escape ...'

Diane says uniqueness doesn't count unless you end up on a monument, and even then the writers get at you and daub your privates – no, it's true you must first start off as women, quite generic, then you take the special path that only you ... and Stark says crossly,

'You just hang by Corinne, Diane. That special path, it lies in her, you're just an entryist ...' and on he talks, of militancies long soured, and revolutions spun away like helium, or twister marbles, of Russians dead, exhumed and spat upon, and so I say,

'Well, I'm the special one, I've been here since time began. Time – you thought you'd invented it! I made my pile – and then away it flew like leaves or mist or dew and mayflies. It promised much, a life of leisured nothing in particular ...' and tears come to my eyes, and Pippa says, 'You spared us work, demeaning as it often is. And now there's none,' but they all look expectantly, and I say,

'I pose the questions, the answers – those are up to you,' and Diane says the work has gone to where industrious guys – they maybe have no special paths – can hoe between the rows and suffocate the fish in streams, and we are silent, for the sadness of it all, and how the wealth it seems to turn to rot, and yet you need it so, to lie upon the grass and sing, and Stark says,

'Yes, bastards, you may sing, but I'm the stupid Damian with the scythe who mows the grass,' and we all laugh and cheer, and then Stark says the secret lies in icons, and he takes the rabbit bones we've sucked and loads them in his pot.

*

'Pippa's quite farouche,' I say to Stark. 'You ought to watch her.' And he says,

'That's what I do, I watch – it does no good. There's enemies, from them you run, or turn and shoot them down. There's plagues of stinging things – with them, you scratch and suffer. But Pippa – she's another thing. One answer is – we make this place an island, break the causeway, leave the mainland. Just us, the castaways. I know there's other coney islands, but it's there the humans breed, and build their pleasure wheels, the ghost trains going round and round, those mirrors that show you what old age will bring, the face all fallen in, the legs quite mortadella, and the eyes enamel plaques ... our island could be different, although ...'

'No, no,' I say, 'here, we've eaten everything. Those Kazakh guys would give us hell – without the causeway how'd they get to work? No one to buy your icons, so, no carrots for the rabbits. Besides, all day we'd have Diane – those gloomy songs! Corinne – the clothing inappropriate: that beaver stole, the pebble glasses – blue ... Imagine it!

'It's true, I've done it once, built, invented

everything, what patience in those intervals when nothing lived, just slime that crawled up trees and ate the leaves. And then – my winning touch, my lucky streak, those guys and gals who begged to work for me and spend their lives to make more wealth, and more and more than I could count or spend or usefully invest – all altruistically on my behalf.' I pause, the immensity, it sucks you in ... and then it spits you out.

Stark says, 'You're crazy! It wasn't you alone, yours was the finger, chancing on the keyboard. That's the truth. Your long shot came right up, but guys who toiled in other stalls alongside – they had their runs of wins, accumulators florid and bizarre ... and then it stopped. It always does. It is a struggle, friend – the good hand and the evil one, they're locked in struggle, that is true. But both the hands are yours – you've seen it done in movies, and in bars, for sure. The same it is with luck – you win, and then you lose. And as for Corinne – you should understand, she doesn't dress, she's dressed. She pays, and every week some guy, he sends a wire to tell her who is who, and what is what, and what to wear. She's just a servant of the new, the retro, or the worn-right-through – whatever that guy fancies, she puts on.'

'I couldn't know,' I say, 'But still, a kermesse on an island, that appeals; could be just right,' but Stark is firm, he says, 'There's contradiction there: if you succeed, then lots of guys will come. We want to keep them out – the balance is the finest thing: to isolate ourselves, and not to starve to death.'

'But,' Pippa says, 'this here is not an island – there's people in abundance, hinterland. Commercial centre too,' and Stark quite crossly says,

'It's just a metaphor, my sweet,' and Pippa says,

'I can tell metaphors – I have a scientific bent.'

I say to Pippa, 'Now's the time you should calm down.'

She says, 'It's just my clothes – they've taken off, all by themselves.' I don't believe her. She's behind it all. Clothes can't behave.

'Of course they can,' she says. 'Look at the history, all the big poppies, they're dressed different, that's how you recognise them. Besides, you're changing too: what is your destiny? – become a stone, a toad, quiet among the wallflowers?'

'I think.' I say: 'I can lie there, in the dust. And the scent is good.'

'Wait,' she says, 'Until the tanks come by. Think you'll scramble up on one? They'll come to free us, or to chase us. Do you have a project then? Shall we be saved? You watch, watch us, but you're observed, for Mr Driver, he's behind us all, we've nothing for him we can trade, for what he want's excessive, never ends. Millions, as you say, but since they don't exist, went into space, it must be something else he seeks.'

'What can that be?' I ask. 'We've had it all, or most: eruptions, the nuclear and 'flu. Hard to protect against all that – and then it all breaks up. Afterwards, it's just the details – houses in flames. All that. And trapped inside.'

I know what Mr Driver wants. He wants to drive, to herd, to push us on, from waterhole to empty bucket. He is the knout. I'd rather use it on myself, if no one else is ready to ... Diane tells us it may serve, the flagellation, private, public – accompanied by bells and garlands. Or just your room, your radio plays to hide your cries.

'Well,' says Diane, 'We can start again from me. I have no prejudice, no grudge.'

'Fuck you, Diane,' Corinne shouts at her. 'Your pretty little mouth, all fresh and clean. You have no weight, no strength, you're glitter-dust,' and Pippa says the problem seems to be – your granddad hanged my grannie, so my dad has walled your mum up in the fireplace, on it goes, and Stark is thoughtful, and he says there's lots of stretches where this sentimental stuff is of no use, there's years when guys make chairs and shoes, and all is quiet. He says,

'The thing is this – a lion has ate my aunt, and when I see another lion, I give it hell. It's just a species thing. Those lions are not related, not one bit. It just turns out that we're a species that's aggressive – to them within as well as those outside who bite and sting,' and Pippa says, 'We get to eat all those ones too, and few of us gets ate.'

'So, here we are again,' says Corinne, 'you're all exasperating. It's good and evil hands, over and over, push and pull, and looking for excuses, flagellating to the numbers, innocents and guilty – will you never stop?'

She's right. We stop.

We start again.

'Quiet, quiet, you clowns,' shouts Corinne. 'It's not about lunch or cockroaches, you trivials. You chatter round and round, you zombies, like you've done for centuries. Battle and peace! You waste your time. Let's go to Diane's ashram, she set it up herself, and there'll be eats, I guess, and maybe revelation too.'

In Diane's ashram there are wicker thrones – the kind that went out years ago, and velvet dogs that could be gods, and lacquers blue and green. She lays down smoke, and there's the space that ought to serve for revelation or at least a small epiphany, and Stark runs out, he shouts, 'I hate these things, they made me cry first time I saw. They said I wasn't pure. The place was dirty anyway,' and Corinne says,

'Diane, you're quite a little bowerbird, my love. But now – I have in mind to kit you out, you lot, and make you a brigade. I'll measure you for uniforms ...' and Diane says,

'Not military please,' and Corinne says brigades can be for work, besides, the measurement's the thing, there are no uniforms.

Diane apologises, seems she'd once a child, a daughter, that she gave away: 'Born in despair, and in despair she went, and ended in despair,' she says, and maybe finished up in someone's regiment, and Corinne says,

'Well, well, I didn't know, we all step from the dark and wait a while before we step back in – besides, what happened to that tiny thing?' Diane says,

'How should I know? It was a choice, we're always being asked to make them, and I did,' and we agree the ashram's got its victims, or its worshippers, maybe both.

Corinne takes all our measurements, but doesn't write them down. She says, 'The fighting's done by robots now, and if they err, there's other robots dressed in wigs that let them off the consequence. It's quite the same with work, you watch the robot doing it – the trouble is, the robot gets your pay,' and we all laugh, and Corinne says,

'It's training time – we'll fly and sail.' She binds our eyes, we sit upon the floor, and there's a whoosh, and Pippa says, 'We're safe upon the ground.' I tell her that's untrue, and start to think that Corinne maybe never governed Denmark, but she shouts above the engine noise, 'There's no drinks or safety stuff, I'll put the music on,' and here it comes, it's great, as if large pearls drop in our ears, and when our brains have pondered it – the chant, it might be, or a passacaglia – our minds have turned to shredded silk, and through our sightless eyes we see the fields of blue and green and velvet dogs, and there's the space where we must land ... and Corinne says, 'Now, it's sailing ships,' and off we go, the ground goes up and down and roundabout, it's our kermesse, but here we are all ghosts and in the sea, all green and black, there's hosts of ghostly mariners, they cry for help but on we go, and Corine shouts,

'Don't stop, don't stop – the wind is ours, you ride it while you can, and if you stop, your breath stops too,' so on we slice through waves and ghosts, and ...

Oh no, it's Mr Driver, and he says, 'You've passed the training, but I fear you could be terrorists – although, Corinne, you have no people following you,' and we cry, 'yes, yes, we're people too,' for we begin to doubt, all sitting hugging close and in the dark, and Corinne says, 'We're bonding, have no fear – the terror, it runs deep within, if we have a nature, it's the being scared. Your terrorism, Mr D, depends on who did what to whom, and when,' and he says no, that's merely vengeance, and she says that no, it is just history, proximate justice's what it's called. Then Mr D says terror's what you feel or make the others feel, what is involved is where you want to go, not where you've left, and we're unsure of what we've left or where we want to go, and Mr D says that's the very worst of terrorism, and Corinne says to him 'fuck you', and that it's time for training more, this time it's fighting and surrendering, so we can stand this time, and look around. And so we do.

'Surrendering – that's the important part to learn,' says Corinne, 'Fighting is easy – it's surrendering doesn't just depend on you.'

'I want pompoms on my uniform,' Diane says,

'And you shall have them, loverkiss,' says Corinne, 'Which brings us to our next – lesson four, on loving, hating, and something in between.'

'I don't know where I stand,' says Pippa. 'Nor on terrorism. I've done nothing ...'

'That's your defect,' says Corinne sharply, 'That's why you've no opinion on anything.'

'I could say I love you all,' says Diane. 'That would be true, but when it's down to individuals, there's hate and in-between.'

'We have to love each other,' says Stark reluctantly, 'Or else we're not well-trained.'

'Do as you wish, fuck you all,' says Corinne. 'The

manual doesn't say. There is a page on love-and-stick, and love-and-run, and counting costs. Then there's a sentence on hating, that comes much easier. Let's pass it over, concentrate on "indifference" ...' but Pippa isn't satisfied and Stark helps out,

'Let's put in culture and contingency.' We all agree, though it's not clear to what, but we must bind and bond, and not just sexually, and Corinne says that's the next thing – a general inter-gender marriage, that is what we need. No one declares their preferences, their bent or twist or trying out – and sex is not the issue here, nor sharing of our property, for we have none, and if we're sick, we take our chance like everyone; then Pippa says that Kazakhs do things right, marrying and festive times,

'But,' says Stark, 'They've got more cash, and parents too, and animals to trade out back,' so they're irrelevant, it seems, we're happy, just as we were before, but married all together now, and Pippa holds my hand and tells me I am free. I say,

'Thank you, Pippa. Being in charge, and debt, that was an awful weight, and making things tick over, even sound the hours.' She pulls away and says no no, that wasn't what she meant: 'You're free to be one of us,' and that's a greater weight, or maybe meaningless.

'Right, you're all as trained as me. Now we can go outside,' says Corinne, 'And if there's sides to take, people to save, and feed, and give them medicines – that we can do as well,' and Stark draws back, and says,

'Outside? No, no, we can't. We always tell the truth. Have you not understood? Truth when we're all together, never when we're on our own. Now, we're a mystic knot, of snakes that writhe but do not bite, and always make the shape, within our basket. There's the altar' – and indeed, we've all along been in the ashram – 'There was no flight, no landing and no sea. Ghosts there were, but after all, who cares about them? Here we all lie, sacred, anointed, consecrated to the cause. We tell the truth, Corinne: no work, no pay. More than that, we cannot say ...' and he could proceed, but Corinne says,

'Snakes have no truth. We're trained to love humanity, but we've our venom too ...' and Pippa says our circle's very small, and not a mystic knot, but just a knot.

'There!' says Corinne, 'I've done what I can.You're all set up. Reserves.'

'Corinne,' says Stark, 'we're useless. Maybe that's the way we want, for sure it's what we know,' but she interrupts, and says, 'No selling short, young Stark, besides, look how there's been so many useful people killed in swathes. Imagine what they'd do to you, the useless ones ... Resist or die, it's up to you, an option –

understand?’

I say, ‘Stark, maybe Corinne is right, it’s true the guys outside – inside – they’ve got philosophy, it says ‘don’t meddle with the useless guys, let’s pretend they’re precious stuff.’ The script is read, the lines are learned, but will they do the play? And get the ending right?’

‘That’s metaphysics, isn’t it?’ asks Stark. ‘I thought I recognised ...’

Good honest plodding Stark. I say, ‘The metaphysicals, you do them once, then leave behind – I don’t concern myself with that, it’s in a different register. Maybe the bats can hear and dodge,’ but he’s deaf too, my jokes bounce off, like bats avoiding walls. He goes on, ‘My passion. With Pippa, I’ve no hope or joy – that’s not what love’s for, they say?’

‘Stark, you have your art, and so unhappiness is probably your best, indeed your only, asset. Do not whine,’ I say.

It’s true that Pippa is a flighty thing, and clinging too, and cracking up, it seems. Now we’re married, all of us, and a brigade, I can’t escape, we all are bound together. Mr Driver, if he wants, could make us go around the world in lockstep. We speak a lot of love. Diane complains that hers is quite the bland, expansive kind, and now she shrinks away when Corinne calls her ‘sparkytongue’ and lays her mottled paw on her.

*

Mr Driver's here again: 'You're in a camp,' he says. 'Trained. In a brigade. That's bad, that's very bad.'

'It's nothing, just to keep our due,' I say.

'Diane's faith, now spinning out, and Pippa's clothes gone feral ... Who's in charge?' he asks.

'I am,' says Stark.

That's a surprise.

'Just pay your debts,' says Mister D. to me.

'It's evident I can't,' I say.

'There's other guys elsewhere that's done it, whole heaps better,' Mister Driver says. 'You guys, you want a paternoster – stepping up and off your ruined planet, on to the new; and dancing. It can not be done, my friends.'

Driver shuffles off, with threats. I explain to Stark, all about love.

'I devised it all myself,' says Stark: 'Pippa, all that.'

'No, no, you can't have done,' I say. 'It's much too complicated, see …' and I explain, love – the sacred, the profane, the pure and not, of God and not, material stuff, and love for things that aren't material, like country, honour, or consistency, or having a good time. For nature, and its pieces – some gone missing – men and women too, their alls, their smell, what you can and can't remember, that you did and want to do again, or maybe not, but still it's on and on ...

'And all that's love?' asks Stark, bewildered.

'Oh no, dear Stark,' I say, 'we're not yet into what it really is, a feeling or a state of mind, or conduct, or a thing you say, having at the time no better thing,' and then Stark interrupts, and says,

'No, no, you're too far from the shore, the thing is losing weight, it has no bones, it's a medusa, it's a thing dissolved.'

I say, 'Well, Stark, that's it. Those are some parts of love. And then there's Pippa, quite another thing ...'

We go our ways, reflecting.

*

Here's Pippa, with her lettuces: she says, 'Stark's crazy – what he feels, he'd like to pin a name on it, but he turns round and round and bites his tail.'

She strokes a rabbit's nose. It could be mine. A gesture quite offhand, but – touch of flesh on flesh: you can't be closer and more intimate than that. There lies a present and a past. I sidle closer, and I say,

'Pippa, I love you.'

She doesn't say a word. What can I do with that? Silence. Nothing. Silence stands between us, raising its infinity of eyebrows. What has that to do with love, I wonder – the eyebrow? A love that I missed out when listing them for Stark: one-sided, or exploratory, love.

A statement.

'Here, you beautiful thing,' she says, pushing lettuce in the rabbit's face. 'Eat and be ate. Enjoy.' It seems the rabbit does.

*

'They call you guys creators – that's a laugh,' Diane says. Maybe I'll get some sense from her, Diane. I say,

'Well, we did create the wealth, and now the poverty. It's Mr Driver's duty now, to push it on. It's true there's lots of us, each in his quadrant, his carrel, but once we set things up, we intervened less often, and now – we, I, don't intervene at all.'

'Your excuses!' Diane says. 'If you're so smart, you could have fitted us with better bodies, that didn't itch and fall apart. Some real things too – not written on a balance sheet of what to eat and where we'll finish up, in red or black, hell or heaven, as you say – yet they all seem much the same ...'

'No, no,' I say. 'What did you dream? The red, the hell, was cool, the flames were just a threat, design. It is no hotter than the here-and-now; and heaven, solvency – that was mansions everywhere, the temperature just didn't enter in. It's gas bills and the pruning you must watch. As for bodies – there's the chain of history that holds you back – not I, nor

Corinne, can do much to ease you in your envelope. That flesh will cling to you until it rots, I fear. You're tied right in to causal chains and time, my dear – not I nor you can have the choice.'

Diane says she's not content: 'Choice? History? To me they're just the same, no difference,' and I am weary, and I say,

'Maybe, maybe, I can't go through that now. The fact is, Diane, if you don't like Corinne meddling with you – dump her quick. That's my advice, and no disputes!'

III

'MONEY from Mr D? Explosives? Blow up the Centre, all those stores? Again? Why should we save this guy, he's just a trader who got stung.' Stark points at me, he shouts; the others, noncommittal, gawp.

I say, 'Just an idea, to get that Mr Driver off my back. We're trained, and as you know, there's money in this terrorism – they spend and spend to buy it off. I know you guys – you're just like everyone. Your destiny is riches, Capital's the path – there's no dispute. But here's the plan ...'

'We've heard the plan,' says Corinne – 'Get cash from Mr D and pay him back with it, and maybe kill some guys ...'

'That part sounds good,' says Stark. 'The babbling crowd is mean,' and there's agreement there.

'It's not our destiny, though,' says Pippa, and she tells us what it is – her scientific bent comes through. She says, 'I left a pan too long upon the fire, it melted down and made a shape that wasn't of the world. That is our destiny – one day the sun will eat us up. Like falling in the fire, hotter than hell ...' and Diane looks quite pale, and says, 'Who'll look after us, take care of us when we are in the furnace, then? – and no, I don't want that it should be you, Corinne,' and Corinne says it's just some nasty tale Pippa's made up, and not to worry, someone will sort it out, and then she points at me, and says, 'Maybe this guy – he's a creative' – 'No!' shouts Stark again. 'He traded, that is all. No riches and no capitalism – that is what he's brought.'

'It makes our destiny sound bleak,' says Corinne, and pinches Diane on the arm, quite hard: 'Maybe we could try terrorism – each one has their convictions and their needs. Ambitions too,' and I imagine governorships are there before her gaze, and then she says,

'Why, look! I think we are attacked,' and up she points – the roof ... and Diane says, 'No, no, Corinne, those are just birds, they live on crumbs, they do not shoot,' but Corinne says they're robots with mechanical ears, that spy on us, and maybe lob a bomb, and we are all exhausted with the discourses that wreathe around.

Diane quietly asks me, 'That's a terrible end, even if we're dead before it all occurs. Do you think the rabbits know?'

'Of course,' I say. 'That's why they don't sing.'

She's silent, then, 'I wonder if Danes sing.'

'Of course they do, though not as much as Lithuanians,' I reassure her.

*

Mr Driver says, 'Now, let's get this straight. Do you want cash to start the terror, or just not to?'

'We're quite exasperated,' says Stark. 'We have our rights and visions too, you know.'

'Mine are the better ones,' says Mr D. 'I know you've heard me say before, but I can prove it – that is where the flow is tending. One value is, you have to pay your debts – even if they're not quite yours, but some of you must have a mate, a partner, take responsibility ...' and he points at me.

'We can't pay,' says Pippa, 'Because we're poor. That's why we have to cheat you. Give us the cash, or let us live according to ...' and she breaks off.

D. ponders long, and says, 'When you are rich, you'll pay me back,' and, 'Yes, yes,' we cry, 'For that is what we want, what everybody wants,' and Corinne says, quite quiet to me, 'I'm sure those Kazakhs deal in guns,' and I am shocked and say,

'Those racial stereotypes, my dear – unworthy of you. Those guys just make the hooch – already that's a breach of all they must hold dear. A Kazakh is the best: you'll never have a better friend,' and she is shamed, helps Mr Driver do his sums, his calculations on our deal.

Diane makes like she's a procession, and she

chants, alone, 'Oh lead us, lead us back ... Into the black ...' She circles round. I ask, 'Where's Corinne's cash? She must have some, with all those clothes ...' and Corinne says, oh no, it's all in crowns, the old ones, made of tin. She lies. She says,

'It's useless to invoke, my dearest ex, your key won't fit my heart, nor yet my safe ...' and through some tears, she triumphs.

Stark pushes forward: 'I've an idea. We'll put on Wozzeck, make some cash ...' and at once Corinne says, 'Yes, Wozzeck. That's my favourite! The Kazakhs will adore it,' Pippa says,

'It's best to fall back on the rabbits. Besides, in Wozzeck – what's the ending?' And Stark says,

'You know it very well. It's all the ending.'

'What's riled you up, dear Stark?' asks Pippa, and I think she starts to cry again.

'We've got the knife,' says Diane, she is thrilled, she loves the rituals, 'Then there's atonement, of a kind – except ... there isn't water here for Wozzeck's drowning ...' and Corinne says we're only amateurs, we can mime the pond, or wave our arms, make river, sea or flood, and Stark says,

'No drownings here. It's just – I'm tired of Pippa, and her science too. Diane has split with Corinne – nothing says I have to stick with this one here,' and he disowns her, Pippa, here and now, like it's a play.

Then I say that we should stick to terrorism, but will we know when we have won or lost? – and Corinne says she'll do the politics and parley when it's time – we only need remember what our training said, and what's our cause, and Mr Driver'll do the same, and history will be our judge, and she will buy the book when it comes out, and lecture too, and Diane says she's read the book, a different one – and Stark picks up the knife ...

'No, no,' I shout. 'Don't leave me here with Corinne and Diane, for you and Pippa, you're supposed to start it off. Plant things, have kids, and do things all a different way.' And he lays down the knife.

*

Here's Driver round again, and Diane says,

'We have rejected terrorism. It's just a tactic, and we haven't got the time to flee and fly, and in the end, there's grumpy people like before ...' and Corinne says,

'No terror, Mr D – we just thought of killing you, and you alone!' and Diane says, 'Mouth! Mouth, dear!' quite automatically.

And Mr D replies, 'Assassination? All a waste of time, my dear – it's all more complicated – not just give and take, accounts, the scarlet and the black, and prices up and down. Look,' he points at me, 'this guy knows quite well – the trading's just a hobby, for the universe was made for Capital, and we must serve it to the end – I fear there is a punishment for non-belief and bolshiness. For at the last, the guys and gals that don't obey will see the sun expand ...'

'Yes, yes,' says Stark. 'We know all that. We are of scientific bents,' and Pippa says,

'It's true we're different shapes and size, but we're the good ones, any killing that is done ...'

'Is done for love,' and Diane finishes our noble thought.

I feel that no one has much love for anyone around, and Mr Driver says,

'I see you've rabbit trouble,' and it's true, some ran away and had their fun, the grass is full of them, all shape and size, and some quite rare, maybe, and Mr D is generous, and says,

'I'll send some hunters in, and give you some more room,' and we are silent. That's not in our plan.

When Driver's left, Stark says, 'We don't want those goddam hunters in. They bring the spies,' and Pippa says that's true, there's bodies left around, and hunters leave unkempt what they can't cut up and eat. Diane says that what is worse, the bodies are of women, some with pieces taken out, and Stark says that there's guys there too, it's always so, you find some land abandoned, and there's always people to be dumped, you find it in the movies and the books – we've heard it all a thousand times, you wave your hands, it doesn't go away, and ...

'It all starts off in basements or in barracks, and we don't have those at all,' Diane says, though she is ready to accuse, and Corinne bristles up, and says, the most Diane would do is set the foxes on the rabbits, then the wolves upon the foxes. On she goes.

'Well,' I say, 'those women, cadavers, is probably contraband or sex. The men – politics, religion. We're protected here – there's Diane with religion, Kazakhs do the smuggling, Corinne is politics – that leaves the maniacs ...'

'That's Pippa,' Stark shouts out.

'Stereotypes again,' says Pippa. 'You think we're protected? Makes no sense at all – whatever is, it's all around us,' and it's true, the shooting's always nearer, like the creeping round, the fear.

'No, no,' I say. 'It's not to do with debts,' but there they go, they chant: 'Lead us, lead us – back into black...' and even Stark is in the ashram, doing penitences.

Yet – there's a rhythm of nature here, supports us, slenderly. There's grass and rocks, mountains that just now are pink. People shouting – could be harvesting, if you could make them out. From everywhere they come. No big animals, but that's a blessing too. We all have tragedies and bandages. There's birds of good wish and ill omen, spaces for the mystery, and for arguments against it. It could all fit a sheet of paper – merely a sketch, some charcoal lines. It's all as good as it could be.

I sleep alone. Diane and Corinne – still quite close but sleeping back to back, two corbies. Stark rolls into Pippa, that's his style, he snores, he maybe dreams or just thinks over.

Diane does the music for our nights – her songs like question marks, quite sweet, as if what will happen to us is some kind of mystery.

IV

IT'S ALL NORMAL. We fit into our functions quietly, like pistons. Stark is normal. He feels betrayed, but no longer homicidal. Suicide is impossible. Unthinkable too, or else the whole project fails.

'Stark,' I say. 'You're sure about the cubs? No progeny? You've been a soldier, I expect, you know how easy it is, overdoing, then off to better things. One shot. Cleaning your arm with one still up the spout,' I laugh, embarrassed: 'That's how they put it. Accidental. End of your line.'

'I was a good soldier,' he insists. 'That is, incompetent, and on the right side. Against the evil ones.'

'That was lucky,' I say.

He asks, 'Why the two corbies, Diane and Corinne? In the song, it was someone else's eyes they went for, not each others'.'

'Oh,' I say, 'don't bring your memory in too much. Just lying there, those two, sleek and dark, quite heraldic. No silly clothes.'

The hunters make a line, they advance, shooting. Little tufts of brown rise up: some are divots, some are rabbits. The legs kick out, they flop. All that engineering, hardly worth it. So soft.

'Pippa's guy in town,' says Stark, 'I guess he's got the beat. Something I never learned.'

'Fuck it all,' I say, 'quit that jealousy. Accept. Rejoice. Follow your destiny. Shut up about it. Paint. Boil your bones.'

'Those hunters give the Kazakhs hell,' says Stark. 'They must be from that agency against the smokes and booze.'

It's all quite normal here. There on the horizon there's some little spurts of natural stuff, flames. Saltpetre – there used to be a toy, a card, you set light to parts of it, inside was tiny fireworks. Here, it's quite the same, but on a larger scale, far off. Stark says,

'Immense, those fires. The burning off.'

*

'You're rather few to have a plan,' Mr Driver says.

'You've no idea,' I say. 'How little cash it takes to start us off. We're trained. We've faith, and food, and art. Just call your goddam hunters off, and we'd have food to hand, just scoop it up ...'

'Talking of cash,' he starts – 'No, no,' I say. 'I'm sure that after work you found discarded millions in our bins. Nothing is lost, it cannot be, it's immaterial, and so it never ends or dies. It circulates. I don't owe anything.'

'Well, you lost your perch,' says Mr D. 'And now

you're driven, like the rest, and you're a heavy beast, roused by the beaters ... it's too late for plans. Up, forever up – flap yourself off, try to escape ...'

'It's tragedy,' I say. 'I thought I'd watch this normal pair, maybe endow their kids – with cash, if not with wisdom ...' and he interrupts,

'You idiot, they won't reproduce, and if they did, their kids won't know you – though they'll spend the cash ... Remember what the great book says, 'Can't buy me love ...' Eternal truth, if not in the short term...' He lectures on.

It's maybe true.

'I'm the one you'd want to be in charge, responsible,' I say.

Pippa and Stark, they've overheard, 'No, no,' they say, 'you're ineffective, and it's best that way.'

*

Corinne and Diane make a trench, to keep the hunters out. It goes all round, they cover it with gorse and stuff.

'For sure, a hunter's going to fall right in,' I say.

'That's the idea!' Corinne says, and then – well, down one goes.

He's held his gun improperly, and as he falls, he shoots poor Corinne in the face.

'Oh no,' says Diane, 'he's laid bare her teeth – look! – how malign she seems, her cheek has gone away. The rose was opening, the pellets – look, we can pour vodka down her throat, bypassing lips and tongue...' and Corinne doesn't speak.

We think, as she's a trooper, that she'd say she doesn't bear a grudge, it's all in duty's way. Or then again, she might just plead for doctors, nurses, all that stuff. It's all of no account – she cannot say, and we all stand around and twist our hands.

Corinne is mute and back in Diane's territory, and Diane says, 'You guys all know of my attachment to the word. The picture too, of course,' she nods to Stark and smiles. 'There is a concrete thing to do for poor Corinne. We'll cancel on the spot that guy who sends her frocks. As things are, she'd only bloody them, besides, it's better to be contrite now, than vain.'

We all agree, when death is at the door, the fiery chariots may come, or they may not, but with some spades you can prepare to dig the graves, and Diane says the poems and the songs for funerals are her domain, and we're relieved. But Mr Driver says we're in a spot, the hunters want revenge, why did we make a moat when walls were what we need, and Pippa says to me, not to stand lunkish but to dig a hole, and Corinne seems to plead, but makes no noise, and so the worst thing's happened and we lighten up: things must improve, as Corinne bubbles out ... Her star implodes...

Diane says, 'I'll sing this song as she goes down:

"Oh, load me into your limousine:
Over the deserts of damascene,
Jade mountains – travel the imperial scene
I'll be the princess, but never your queen ..."'

'Where does Corinne come in?' asks Mr Driver.

'It's an individual song, not a personal one,' says Diane huffily: 'It's just about moving on and being one's own.'

There's a slight scratching. Corinne with a nail, here's a tile, it says, 'I'm not dead.'

'What can that mean?' asks Mr Driver.'At such a sad time, too.'

'We never knew her well,' says Pippa. 'And if she's not dead, it's harder. No easier, certainly.'

'Probably Danes knew her better,' I say. 'Though I don't see why, or what significance it has. And – Diane, damascening doesn't work for deserts: it's incision, not a surface,' and Diane says crossly, 'That's exactly what I meant. You haven't the poet's eye, you just want to be sung to. So, there you are.'

'Look,' says Mr Driver, 'there's lots of ways to look at things, I know, but you guys are at your edge. Those hunters won't retreat. They'll bring the heavy guys. They'll punish you and then rejoice. You strayed. You sinned.'

Stark says, 'We'll give Corinne good burial – now or later, when it serves. And find a better song. And we're agreed, knowing her or not – it doesn't mean a thing. She lives, she dies. And that is it! No limousines, Diane – stick to your quest,' and Pippa says,

'The funeral meats – it's dogfood, guys. Those hunters, they have finished off the living food, it's maybe being canned and that is what we'll eat,' and Corinne bandages her face, the food goes down her throat, direct. We look away, a dead guy at the feast is sad, but things will now improve, the worst has surely passed.

'Fuck you all,' Corinne scratches: 'I'm not dead.'

Mr Driver says, 'Crisis over! I'll take charge, but don't think that you're safe. I've two daughters, and I'm in the naval reserve, an officer. I don't keep up with fashionable ideas ...'

'This guy is strange,' says Stark. 'He says our island here, within the moat, is called the Isle of Ancient Dreams, but that's all gone and done. The Island of Kermesse – now, that sounds good; that, I prefer,' and Diane says we need to make a face for Corinne, tortoiseshell would suit her well, a gold shield for the nose, or brass at least. The mouth down in the throat – an orifice is better unadorned ... and we ignore her. Angrily she says,

'If no one listens, then I'll be like her, be mute. No other word you'll hear,' and that is how she does.

'Mister Driver tells his life, curriculum, to show he's boss,' I say. 'It's not to show humanity.'

'You bet he's got crap jobs lined up for us,' says Pippa. 'The plough, the vine, and shovelling smelly stuff – it's classic, but he doesn't see, a history of the future doesn't constitute a plan,' and Stark says crap jobs aren't about the future, and there's never been a plan, the future's just about a going on and on. Even those ancient dreamers would only sit around and sing all day ... Pippa says that's what we do now, and Stark says planning's quite impossible, we're a species open-ended and we're vulnerable, there's hunters all around... Maybe no future and no plan.

Pippa pinches me and says it's all my fault. I say,

'I wondered when you'd come to that. My fault I came, and then to lose the wealth, still worse! Chase me away, like Oedipus! Add murder, incest to my score,' and Pippa says they'll do just that, Diane will claw my unbelieving eyes, I'll be a sideshow ... Kermesse Island – that's my destiny.

'If it's to be a kermesse, it needs a wheel,' says Pippa. Stark laughs, and says Corinne was a big wheel, punctured now – who'd pay to see her ruined face?

Pippa says that people pay to see their feet: 'It's the obesity,' she says: 'Corinne is done up fine. The motif "I'm not dead" could be an installation, just write it over everything,' and Diane breaks her silence, says there's not much where it could be chalked, and Stark says no one will come anyway, to ride the wheel, and see the grass and sky, commercial centre – they would have to leap the moat.

'You idiots!' I shout. 'That's the attraction. The great leap. In a day or so you'll make my missing millions back, and we'll have come full circle. There's your wheel!' I say, and they're impressed.

*

'Pippa,' I say, 'I'm not as tranquil, pastless, as you think. I've seen it all, abundance of Pippas passing by, and most have healed. They're all alive, here, behind this wall – you hear them softly speak. They all start off again, new, from the same place.'

'I hadn't thought,' she says, 'or thought about you. We just came here to camp, protesting, now we're here for life. For me, it's just experience – we have it, and it's gone. Nothing left: no monuments are left.'

'Those monuments, they get pulled down,' I say. 'Now, Diane's the rancid one. And when she finds her path, you bet we'll have to follow her.'

'No, no,' says Pippa. 'Kermesse is maybe rough and cruel, but when you leave, it doesn't follow you. You pay, is all. They say it's fun, a whirling up and down, distortion, aiming with bent guns. We just oversee the trade, the tickets. Diane – she's just fluff. Don't be concerned.'

'Pippa, you're wrong,' I say. 'We can't leave. When we set up our sideshows, we are in them for eternity.'

'Relax,' she says, 'There's no eternity.'

'Pippa,' I say, 'whatever's wrong with Stark, you are the one he clings to – you're his stick.'

'I hope when we have set our kermesse up,' she says. 'We still can make the leap and leave.'

'So, if you leave,' I say, 'your eyes are just the same, for ever, everything comes in alike, perception doesn't change.'

'I told you, there is no "for ever",' Pippa says: 'Now, with Corinne – should we prop her up or lay her down?' and Corinne reaches for a tile, and Pippa says,

'Yes, dear, we know.' She turns to me, 'My, how she eats, just shovels in – it's a good argument for putting people down, I guess – the food.'

'Perhaps she hankers for a funeral in a boat,' I say. 'When it's the time, of course. Her culture, so aggressive, going down at last. After Denmark, after her, what will arise? The world? All the other cultures?

She had her way once with them. Now you can hear their sound, all over.' But we can't. Only faint ragas, far away and in our minds.

Pippa says, 'We waited long for someone, now you've turned up. It doesn't seem much different. Stark ... well, he walked the world, and now he's tired. Just daubs and such.'

'No, no,' I say, 'we'll make a spectacle, down in a blaze. The lights, the wheel, plush toys. Corinne's boat – now, that's a puzzle, here we have an island with no water. Maybe we can find an empty box ...'

But then I think – away with the Danish stuff, the burning boats, the dithering and the soldiers, ghosts and snapdragons, more drownings. Let's go out with dignity. No tall tales – Danes, Lithuanians, Russians. I know all about you! Aloud, I say to Pippa, 'No heroics, Pippa. I was there, in history, defending my millions, it was ugly. I'm here now, and you want it prettied up, everything. Tiptoe, Pippa, don't fall in the ha-ha, keep your safety on. How can I keep you pure, my dear?'

She doesn't listen. She's looking for a coffin for Corinne.

Stark is painting his wooden blocks. 'The way is to make them dull,' he says, 'and not commercial. Even for the Kazakhs. They've got cash. But for the cash, they sell me booze. It's easier to go on painting till I stop.'

'Love too,' I say. 'That seems quite arid for you.' I laugh, but he says, 'It's anger. Clinging on and being right. That's what I've got.'

Pippa defends him, holding up some wooden slabs, with figures pushing through the glue. She says, 'I see these in a gallery,' and Stark says, 'Yeah – a shooting gallery. We'll give them as a prize.'

'Come on Stark,' I say. 'You can't aim at integrity and self pity too,' but Pippa turns on me, and shouts, 'You! You weren't very nice when you were in charge. And – really, in charge you weren't. But now, where are you?' and she screams again, 'Where are you? Once, dispenser of good things and bad – but things at least!'

'Enough,' I say. 'If you can't love me, let alone your Stark – why should I give you things?'

'Here's Corinne,' says Pippa. 'And let's hear – Roll Up!'

Corinne's magnificent – red-wattled is one cheek, dark shell the other, set off with her brazen beak. Diane rocks to and fro, her path has led inside. It has no destination – 'Yet,' says Diane, sullenly, 'what a fate, Corinne's, to bring her genius to Denmark – another of the melancholic lands, the buildings like the boxes TVs come in.'

'A fairground needs some things to sell,' shouts

Pippa, banging on her drum. 'But we are bored with things. So do without,' and so we do.

Mister Driver comes, inspects: 'You use resources well,' he says, looks down in Corinne's eyes, sees long arcades of fury, and the dark. He says, 'Some fairgrounds have the crazy cars and animals. You're doing well without – they're dirty things, it's best to leave them be. Corinne's a rare Phoenician queen, exploit her – and the wheel as well. I know that's just a metaphor so far, but two attractions – well, eccentric it may be, but that's your charm. Of course, we have our sweet religious fan,' and he stirs Diane, who's keening on the floor: 'But she is for the special tastes, while Corinne makes appeal to all – a warning and a lift.'

He polishes her nose-guard on his overcoat, and says to me, 'You're still a shifty type; says one thing, then another. But I and all the other drivers think you can be used. Made whole again.'

I say, 'You drivers, leave us be!'

He says, 'It's true, together all we drivers make up a kind of personality. But now – you're worthless, and have no fear, we have no big boss enforcing things, we're just a collectivity. Go ahead, and if you make some cash, I'll call some more.' And off he goes.

Soon, Diane says: 'We must find her a way out. Corinne. So angry, under those arcades.'

'No, no, absolutely not, Diane,' says Pippa. 'You

absolutely must not kill Corinne. She is our livelihood.'

Then Stark rouses himself – 'No, Pippa! No, Diane! I'll not be complicit, not with either,' and at once Pippa changes. 'You're right, Stark. It's me, I'm the trouble, I'm not sensitive enough for you.'

Stark says, 'I made you so. Then it would be my fault.'

He's humming, 'My love is a deep blue sea' – how he does go on about love, or maybe it's just the music that he knows.

Pippa says, 'There! You didn't even invent that song.'

Corinne lies like a twisted rope. She looks as if she's winking at us, scowling too. Her hands are going, as if she's searching out a keyboard, an organ sound perhaps, the feet trampling in the devil's register, you hear the mechanisms, opening and shutting like fish mouths.

'Dance, my poor love,' Diane says. 'It's fine. No one will see your wound. Or if they do, everyone expects it, you must make huge movements, on a huge stage.'

'She's really moribund,' says Pippa. 'What will she do? Her new condition, dead. What shall we do, what's the point of starting off, and handing out the tickets?'

'It's what we must,' says Stark. 'It is the something that we do, or else ...'

'Crap,' says Pippa, flylike, zooming round again and skimming off our noses. 'There's nothing left, she's not a question any more.'

'She trained us,' Diane says. 'We can defend ourselves.'

We're silent. It doesn't seem convincing.

*

The Kazakhs look us over, Corinne too. They're unimpressed, they say, 'We've cities full of statues made of solid gold.'

Stark says, 'That's true. But what is that to do with us?'

Pippa says the Kazakhs think Stark's icons look alike. The same. The figure, struggling under glue, the red a wisp.

'Of course they are,' says Stark. 'They're all the same, or similar. That's why they'll all be given out as prizes. That's my point, I try and try to get one right.'

'And if and when you do,' I ask. 'What then? Give up?'

'It could be even that,' he says. 'For when you reach the point, there is no further.'

Diane is shouting at Corinne, 'Open them, your

goddam eyes. And look at me!' The eyes are open, I suppose, they're two barred black doors, behind is dark and fury still, and Diane batters at them, scratches to get inside.

'No, no,' says Pippa, desperately. 'Stop her!' Diane is tearing up some sacred books and makes a wad that looks it could be used to stopper up poor Corinne's throat.

'Fuck you, old crow,' she screams. 'Open your eyes! Communicate! Tell me the secrets, if there are!'

But Corinne cannot speak, perhaps she cannot see. Then there's a cry that comes from somewhere down inside, one bottled up and saved, the moment that she leaves. What can it be, the last lament, the protest, '*fascisti!*', some kind of whistle, express train heading for a crash? ... or just a belch that rids the gut of us, of Denmark, all that past, the flesh, the hope, a yawp – and here's Diane, now with the Kazakhs' hooch aloft – a bottle in her hands, she pours it down inside poor Corinne, fills her right up, some bubbles out, it steams, it disappears.

'There, there,' Diane shouts. 'Happy at last! Die and take our love and hate with you, Corinne!' Maybe she does – at least she's dead.

*

'That's what Diane found, with all her meditation,' Pippa says: 'And Stark and I, we're just two lumps, it seems – and now Corinne's a third, we'll lay her out, quite lifelike here upon these planks.' They stare at me: a speech? a tear? do they want that? Some retribution?

I say, 'I'm the closest to a father you two will ever have – but you're not stiffing me and putting me on show like her! You know, you nearly are my children,' and I try to suck them in. Pippa says,

'All that cash! Not just mansions, but bad, terrible things. You! – and it's all written down! Done, and didn't think.'

'I guess,' I say, placating. 'Far from your perfection, Stark.'

'I'm not there,' says Stark, 'but I shall.'

'Yes!' Pippa says, 'of course you will!' And I think, no, Pippa, no, don't go on and talk of perfection, where you've got to with your bondage guy ... Forget Diane and her cadaver. My history? - I was only an employee, like we all were and almost all still are. Death and the funfair – just concentrate on that.

V

LATER, Stark says, 'We're not so bad here,' and Diane agrees,

'I'm fine now. We'll say Corinne was drunk. In any case, I'm fine.'

We all are fine, and lots more things will happen, and we'll still be fine.

Stark talks of his wheel – 'You see, the sun, it's round, it wheels around. And we sit here, the island's round … it's on the earth ...'

'Yes, yes,' says Diane, 'but Stark, if you go on like that, your wheel – they'll say it's just a metaphor of round and round. You seek perfection, that is something else. You know the sun will rise: tomorrow, even afterwards. But what you want is "going on",' and Pippa says,

'Going on and getting warm.' For it is dark and cold. I say,

'And if we light a fire, who knows who'll come? If we make some cash, Mister D will take it, then there's tax to pay. We shall be integrated, join the rest, as ...' and Pippa makes a face. I go on, 'Inspectors. Or soldiers.'

Diane says she's not afraid, she gathers up Stark's tablets, though he says, 'I'd hope to make a long house out of them,' but what a flame they make, they crackle and they sing, and he's amazed, 'Yes, yes, pictures should make a joyful sound,' he says. The flames race upwards, there's a smell of rabbits eaten long ago, and feasts, and here we are, amidst the glue and wisps of figures all picked out in red, and Diane shouts,

'There, there! See through the smoke – you see the steel, the tunics fringed with bone, raincoats, boots,' and on she goes, and waves her arms and screams, till Pippa says,

'There's nothing there, Diane,' but she's afire, she scatters round the icons, and –

'Oh no!' says Stark. 'You've set us all alight,' Diane, she doesn't understand, and shouts,

'Yes! Burn with a holy flame, and we'll be pure and hollow as a bone,' but Stark is right – the island burns, the moat is full of something volatile, it throws up spars of blue and red, they twinkle like the stars, and Pippa says,

'Oh no! The Kazakhs! Our security, the ditch, the moat – they filled it up with spirits. That way they make tequila, mescal too, matured, coloured – and it's the special kind, with worms.'

'No, no,' shouts Diane, 'it's soldiers – see the arrows and the bombs! Run, run, escape, I'll hold the island' – and we run. We leave security, and we race like dogs. We overleap the ha-ha, and the flames go through and through, 'Heat – yes, it's like the sun,' Stark shouts, but we're quite burnt, the flames – they make an arc, a dome, and Diane sings and shouts, it makes it seem she's many more, it's organs in the deepest register, and sounds of pedalling and staircase falling through, and still she sings, 'Hoyaa, hiyaa ...' It's a triumph Corinne heard in Denmark, when the dark time comes and round the fires they leap and throw each other in, and destiny is at the fringe, and you accept it or you don't, but if they throw you down and burn you up, you've little choice ...

We see Diane, she is magnificent, she burns, her hair stands out like snakes that's flaming, bright phosphorous in water; she sings, her voice burns through and down, down it goes, down through the bass line, to a place we've never heard before. The ground is trembling, as she roars, she terrifies, she terrorises, 'Yes,' cries Stark, 'That is the terror, the voice that sinks below the line, that is divinity, Diane at the last – she's found, she's realised ...' and as we wait for him to stop, we see the fire has reached Corinne, her corpse rears up, all the muscles tensed, her hands flap out, we see the eyes crack open, those black pupils bloom, open like nutshells, and we see long corridors of white, white ladies pushing medicines or maybe flowers, her nails are scarlet, then they're blue like mussel-shells, and now they're black, and she is black, but with her face, her throat, quite sutured up with fire ...

'I come, I come,' shrieks Diane, from the deep she clambers up four octaves, and she screams, 'My love, you sacred bitch, at last, at last, our destiny!' and Pippa says it isn't making sense, but Stark says what can you expect, she's all consumed, and Pippa says, how sad about the mescal, that has been her favourite, and the worms will perish too, just like the rabbits ...

The fire's historic. If the soldiers come, there's nothing left for them. Two cinders, that is all, no need to bury them ... there's rabbit bones all round, and far below a chorus without words rumbles into tiny quakes.

VI

PIPPA says to me, 'Really, I'm with the other guy, not Stark, who's such a weight! A hayseed.'

It's breaking up: sad, after many awful things – the accidents turning into immolation, Diane misleading or misled, the island – nearly a sacred place, and empty now, until the bugs come out and nature starts again.

Pippa says, 'We're all bound to work for Mister Driver. That is what he says. That we should go quite seriously into the circus business.'

'I've nearly got the wheel,' says Stark. 'It could be eye or mouth.'

Pippa says, 'I'll sell the tickets, that is all, enough. Service before everything, that is what they say, no more big plans.'

I say, 'Well, if you won't tread my path, I guess I'll take my gift and start off somewhere else.'

Stark doesn't care: he says, 'We'll send you off. A party. My birthday's here. I'm twenty, looking less.'

Some years have gone that didn't count. I'll go to Ethiopia. Take a packet of seeds. Find a couple, embracing, follow them. I say,

'You've disappointed me, the living and the dead. I'll search for trade and riches – it doesn't matter where you are, or if you're human. Just plug in. It's true – those accidents have brought us down – the context was unpromising.'

Pippa asks, 'Should we have the Kazakhs to the party? We're dependent on their booze. They've made a joy of Coney Island, as they call it now – one part is rigour. Prayer – a tile remembering Diane, scratched out, it must have been, by Corinne. A shrine. The other part – excess and entertainment. Animals – the lot. The little carts, the shooting.'

'No,' I say, 'we're not their scene. No party for those guys. And – Pippa, you're a lovely person – if I could turn you into something more presentable, it would be a tree. Not an animal, of course, and surely not a rabbit. Rabbits will return to where we were. The design is good.' I go on, 'We made some conquests in our time!' I can't remember which: 'We had some courtly moments: even made a calendar.'

Should we invite Mister D, and Pippa's lover? Mr D – we wrote each other off. No, neither of them, but those foreign Mr D's, they have fine manners ...

'May you live another twenty years, may they be long ones,' I say to Stark.

Something ferments inside. It's jealousy. He turns to Pippa, then –

He beats her, his great hands slapping inconclusively. Wiping her face away. He shouts,

'You're leaving, Pippa? Then something of mine you'll take with you!'

It's not clear what – the blood is Pippa's, after all. A memory is all of him she has to take.

'Stark, be reasonable,' I say, but Pippa cries. She says,

'No, no, no happy ends. No happy ends,' and that's quite deep, the best thing she has said, perhaps, and Stark cools down and says, 'Well, there's another conquest, a freedom gained – an interlude of rest for Pippa, somewhere between me and that other guy,' but he's an optimist – that other guy was always there, for otherwise we'd have some freedom all the time, causes, effects would be unglued, and where would we be then? I think, but do not say all this.

Pippa shouts, 'You're waste!'

I say, 'Stark, now that is done, the breaking Pippa up, you'll surely say you've made your round, at last, the wheel. Is it a mouth? Is it an eye? The word? The vision? Certainty or quest?'

'Maybe it's a nose,' says Pippa, holding hers: 'That's a hole, and empty too, just air comes in and out.' And Stark is not appeased, and not amused. He says,

'Fuck the wheel.'

Pippa leaves. We miss her. That is all.

'Well, Stark,' I say. 'A party with us two. It is a

time of lamentations. What now of everything outside? Give thought to that – the coups d'état, tall buildings taller, runners ever faster, famine, social classes whirl and crumble – starlings with the miracle of swirl – you see them making cones and rhomboids, like black flies uncounted, all related, clans.'

He's indifferent to starlings. He's nowhere he can park his wheel.

He says, 'I could lament, but after all, there is no intervention, so no point. I could curse you, or kill you with this four by four – but what's the sense?'

'I see that as your limit, Stark,' I say: 'Protest is often called for. Things are not all accident.'

He isn't satisfied. He's right.

He stands, stretches. The darkness lifts. He says,

'There is the Sun! It's rising. As I knew it would.'

Rome, 2012

About the author

John Fraser has lived in Rome since 1980. Previously, he worked in England and Canada.

www.ingramcontent.com/pod-product-compliance
Lightning Source LLC
Chambersburg PA
CBHW020551310726
48979CB00008B/1169/J
* 9 7 8 0 9 5 7 2 0 6 1 1 3 *